Heather was consumed by a terrible guilt

When she had angrily confronted her fiancé for dating another woman, Frederic had stormed out to his car in a blind rage. The fatal car crash was inevitable....

Heather was heartbroken. Time might ease the pain, she told herself despairingly, but nothing could erase her guilt. If only she hadn't spoken so harshly to Frederic!

When she met Anton, she didn't expect to respond so emotionally. But Heather knew that she wasn't free to love again—until she learned the frightening truth about Frederic's death.

Other

MYSTIQUE BOOKS

by CLAUDETTE VIRMONNE

Voices of Terror

by CLAUDETTE VIRMONNE

MYSTIQUE BOOKS

TORONTO · LONDON · NEW YORK
HAMBURG · AMSTERDAM · STOCKHOLM

Prologue

The old woman sat rigidly upright in the dark. Trembling, she drew the bedclothes around her thin, frail body. Her eyes stared in terror at the old dark cupboard. In the night shadows the carved wood seemed to take on life; to twist into strange shapes; to glower at her.

And it whispered. It murmured.

The noises that came from it seemed to echo from some evil ghostly past. They came from far away, like cries of pain, and yet they were close, like demon mutterings right here in this room. In this room—behind those carved doors.

The sounds came and went, and the old woman's terrror mounted.

Then the pain came. The terrible, wrenching pain that paralyzed her limbs and made her gasp for breath.

Choking, she tried to cry out. But she could not.

There was mercy in the blackness that descended on her then, for she felt no more, saw no more. Now she was unable to hear the ghostly sounds.

The old woman was dead.

Chapter 1

The metallic gray sports car rolled smoothly along the mountain road, hugging dizzy curves and steep grades with effortless power. The car's top was down and the bright sun of early summer tossed spangles of light from the metal surfaces.

The breeze that tossed the driver's dark hair was pungent with the resinous perfume of the alpine forest. Dense, cool and mysterious, the trees marched upright on the mountain's rugged slopes until they met high pastures of snow. The mountain peaks were ghostly white, etched sharply against a flawless blue sky.

Heather Ashly was at home among these forbidding towers of stone: *Eiger, Moench, Jungfrau.* They were the buttresses of a fortress to her, symbolizing the safety of her childhood. Here in Switzerland she could seek shelter from the pain of her recent memories; she could begin, perhaps, to forget. But she must not let that intrude now. She was comfortable at the wheel of the little car that she'd purchased in Paris, maneuvering it gracefully along a highway she'd known for much of her life, willing her mind not to think about the past few weeks.

Deliberately, she focused her attention on the road and the familiar landmarks as they came into view. She was struck as always by the clarity and purity of the mountain air. Fragrant with evergreens and wild flowers, it seemed to dance with light, with the very joy of life itself.

Heather felt a tightening in her throat: the joy of life had been robbed from her by Frederic's death. They had arranged to meet in Paris where they were to be married. The pain flooded back, relentlessly. If only she hadn't argued with him, hadn't made those cruel, hysterical accusations . . . .

The black memories ran through her mind with sickening, slow-motion familiarity . . . Frederic storming out of the hotel, leaving her alone with the echoes of her own terrible words. If only she could take them back!

You must stop this, stop blaming yourself! She heard her mother's voice, sensible and soothing. But how could mother *know*? No one knew that along with the shock and loss she felt at Frederic's sudden death, Heather carried with her that most terrible of burdens: *guilt*.

And her mother had been dubious, too, about Heather's plan to come to Switzerland.

"But you *met* Frederic in Switzerland," mother had said. "Don't you think it's a little too soon? Why not go somewhere that isn't filled with associations?" she had suggested gently. "Heather, you're twenty-two; you have lots of time to start over. I know you and Frederic planned to live in Switzerland but . . . . why not consider returning home to Boston? You could go back to school and finish your studies, then think about what you'd like to do."

"But mother—you're forgetting. Aunt Rachel's

house is full of the best *possible* associations—I've
loved the place ever since I could remember. I'm
grateful that you came to Paris during this time, but I
have to go on with my plans, even though . . . ."

"Yes, I know, dear." Mother's eyes had held a
faraway look for a moment. Some of her own
happiest days had been spent in the little Swiss
town tucked away in the Alps; Sion was out of the
reach of the tensions of the big business world
her husband had loved so much.

Her daughter, Heather, had been born in her
Great-Aunt Rachel's house, while she and her young
husband had been visiting there.

They had spent many summers with Rachel
Savorin, a rather stern old lady whose husband
had left her very well-off indeed. Rachel had loved
Switzerland and the clear air of the mountains. It
was natural enough for her to remain there in the
little town after her husband's death.

For the beautiful old house meant more to her
than anything in America ever could. Originally
from Boston, Rachel had come to think of herself
as Swiss—as indeed she was, for she had
renounced her American citizenship years before.

Besides, Aunt Rachel had always said, there were
those ridiculous American tax laws. Sheer nonsense. In a country such as Switzerland they had
sense enough to leave you alone, let you keep your
money.

Yes, it had been altogether more agreeable to
Aunt Rachel to live here among these mountains.
And these orderly people.

I've always felt at home here. Heather realized
suddenly as she rounded a sweeping arc of
roadway and began the descent into the valley of
the Rhone. *It's going to be agreeable to me, too. I
know it, somehow.*

No, under the circumstances this was the wisest thing to do. She could always go back to Boston later to finish her university degree. She wouldn't have been able to concentrate anyway. Mother had only been trying to help her when she suggested coming home, and Heather had deeply appreciated her concern. But in this instance she had to follow her instincts. Aunt Rachel's home offered her the peace and solitude she now wanted so desperately.

The sports car glittered in the late sun. Heather carefully negotiated the hairpin curves of the highway as it descended into a broad valley. On each side of the road deep ravines of spruce forests dropped away. As the valley deepened she could see the patchwork landscape widen below her. Heady scents of wild thyme and lavender filled the air.

It was almost dusk now, and a light mist was rising, swirling softly over the farmlands and the small herds of sleek, Swiss cows that wandered slowly homeward.

Then, in the broad alp-cradled valley with its terraced vineyards and smooth running river, the town of Sion materialized like something from a fairy tale. The majestic fortresses of Tourbillion and Valère stood guard, high on their rocky cliffs, and Heather's heart leaped to see them again

In Sion, under those venerable palaces, centuries of history and tradition blended. The ancient streets once echoed to pageantry and medieval pomp. Nowadays they formed a busy market center.

On this June day Heather drove past stalls laden with strawberries and asparagus: the pride of the Valias.

As she drove into the main marketplace of Sion with its narrow sidewalks and winding streets,

Heather slowed down to look around. The friendly faces of the villagers and the resonant booming of the church bell seemed to fill her with a feeling of peace. She began to relax for the first time in weeks and felt an odd sense of well-being.

She was glad she had come. She belonged here. And legally, it was her house now; Aunt Rachel had willed it to her, as if she knew only Heather truly appreciated it.

From her open car she could hear snatches of conversation between the villagers who called back and forth along the streets. How good it was to hear again the rolling accents of the Valais! She had visited Sion only once in the past ten years, and that had been for just a few days. Heather drove on, taking in the lively activity around her, watching the shopkeepers draw up their awnings for the night.

They were changeless, these Swiss. They delighted in commerce and hard work; and in such a prosperous town as Sion, there was always plenty of cheerful activity.

Heather wondered if she would encounter anyone she knew. She'd come to know a few of the townspeople by sight . . . over there—surely that was Oscar Caron, the good-natured old handyman who'd always taken care of Aunt Rachel's house.

But Heather had no opportunity to wave at Oscar, for a sudden movement just ahead forced her attention back to driving. With her heart in her mouth she slammed on the brakes, narrowly missing a tall, broad-shouldered man.

He drew back, startled, and glared at Heather with unfriendly eyes. She would not soon forget that thunderous frown.

"Why don't you watch where you're going?" he snapped. The question required no answer. It was a steely dismissal in fact, for the man strode on across the street, without a backward look.

Heather sank a little lower in the driver's seat suddenly feeling faint. She *had* been in the wrong. One didn't just cruise through stop signs. She had very nearly hit him.

She stared at his tall, rangy figure as he walked away through the crowds of last-minute shoppers. He was probably a climber, thought Heather, noting his lightweight jacket and heavy boots. His outfit was not unusual even here in the valley. The Mountains ringed the horizon, and distances to the most rugged trails were short.

But why hadn't he at least allowed her to apologize? *Well, I hope I don't run into him on some dizzy mountain face,* Heather mused, shifting into gear. She caught a last glimpse of the man in the side mirror as she pulled away. *Not very pleasant,* she told hereself. *Not an auspicious welcome at all.* Still, it wasn't likely she'd see him again.

She knew her way around town very well. Although square modern buildings had sprouted on its outskirts, the old town was almost exactly as she remembered it from childhood days spent with her great-aunt. She turned left. The little cobbled street wound around, following the ramparts built in medieval days, until it led at last to Aunt Rachel's street.

Heather pulled up in front of the gray stone house.

Here it was. Her second home; her real home. Aunt Rachel would not be there to greet her this time, she thought with a pang of sadness. But Rachel had been old; her life had been good. And her indelible presence marked on this house could be nothing but good, as well.

Heather took her time getting out of the car. She seemed to be moving in a dream. She sat bemused, thinking about Aunt Rachel and the hourless days they had both enjoyed so long ago. She would run through the hallways, brightening them with her awkward clatter, her childish shouts. And Aunt Rachel would pretend to be severe with her, before taking her out to the garden for a lengthy discussion of the roses that grew there in a dizzy profusion.

Or they would read together. Aunt Rachel loved old tales—fairy stories and myths. She would make them come spookily alive for Heather, rolling the well-loved phrases, and making elaborate sound effects. A peculiar old lady, some would say. She kept to herself a good deal, and was very nearly a recluse in her final years. But there had always been something a little bit odd about her.

Like this house, Heather thought, surveying its uneven aspect. Her great-aunt and the strange old house had shared a similar aspect. Neither quite fitted into the comfortable orderly neighborhood, although each had a right to be there.

The house rambled disjointedly on a little slope; it was actually two adjoining structures. In the last century, a "modern" addition had been made to the solid old place, erected no doubt by some prosperous burgher. The older, lower section was now unused and had been virtually empty for as long as Heather could remember.

She did remember, as a child, creeping into that forbidden territory to play silent games sparked by the old legends that were connected with the house. The dim chambers echoed for what seemed like great distances, and to Heather they had been peopled with ghosts of medieval knights, Renaissance bishops, and Roman soldiers—all of whom had passed through the valley of the Rhone in centuries past.

People said, in fact, that originally the old house must have been a mill, then been converted and added to several times. If you looked carefully at its outer walls you could see the work of different stonemasons; but if was difficult to say where old mortar and stone ended, and additions began.

Yet the most recent addition was clearly obvious. More regular, more exactly designed, its eaves swooped down from several high, pitched gables, and these were carved with fine carpenter's gingerbread.

Now, in the deepening dusk, the gables stood out sharply against the sky. Here and there a window glowed yellow, and the stonework was shadowed in uniform blue gray. Heather sensed something subtly different about the place. It had an air of brooding, almost of waiting. But that was silly, Heather told herself. Any building could look mysterious at this dusky hour.

Resolutely, she swung her bags out of the car and climbed the steep, uneven stone stairway that led to the front door. The heavy brass knocker was cool to her touch. She banged it once, twice, then stood eagerly waiting, her heart fluttering with anticipation.

Heather didn't know Celine, the housekeeper mentioned by Aunt Rachel in her last few letters. The woman had remained after her great-aunt's death, because Heather, through her lawyer, had requested her to stay on. It had seemed a sensible arrangement and Heather had been informed that the woman was pleased to continue maintaining the old house.

Now, Heather was rather anxious to meet Celine. What would she be like? Perhaps a broad, kindly Swiss with plump, competent hands? Or maybe she would be very tiny, quick and efficient. Her great-aunt hadn't told her much about the woman.

The moments ticked by very slowly. The dusk had deepened and Heather felt rather forlorn standing on the stone step in front of the silent door. She reached up to bang the knocker again, but the brass slipped from her hands and flopped with a dull clicking sound. The door had at last been opened.

A dark silhouette stood between Heather and the lighted hall within. Disconcerted, Heather stumbled a little over her words.

"Good evening—I . . . I'm Heather Ashley. My lawyer wrote to you, I hope?"

As Heather's eyes became accustomed to the light, she scrutinized the figure in front of her. Angular and graying, the woman was dressed entirely in black. Her eyes were heavily lidded, but Heather could see she returned the intensity of her gaze.

"Yes, he wrote. My name is Celine Dumas," said the woman. Her voice was dry and precise, and entirely without warmth.

Heather was chilled by the way she stood, almost as if she were blocking the door. She fought to overcome the feeling.

It's just that I'm finding it weird to have a stranger here in Aunt Rachel's house—in my house, she told herself.

"May I come in?" Heather smiled brightly. After all, the woman was a servant in her employ!

"Yes, of couse." Celine Dumas stood aside to let Heather in, quietly relieving her of one of the suitcases. Heather's own footsteps sounded strangely loud against the polished tiles of the floor. Celine was following her along the hallway, but the woman's footsteps were silent—almost stealthy. Heather tried to quell her mounting unease.

It was absurd! The woman was just a little bad-mannered, that was all. Heather tilted her chin high and made her way quickly toward the book-lined sitting room, where she had spent so much time. This, in an indisputable way, was hers. She plunked the case down and turned to Celine with an air of confidence.

"Well, here I am at last! I've had such a long trip—from Boston to Paris, and then all the way to Sion by car! And the traffic on the Geneva highway—you wouldn't believe it!"

The sharp-featured face was an impassive mask. "Oh, yes, miss—it's that way this time of year," said Celine. "I've made up Mrs. Savorin's old room for you. Shall I take your bags up?"

"Yes, thanks." Heather smiled again, but this time the warmth was a little forced. The woman did not smile in return. Heather was at a loss for something else to say. She felt small and somehow idiotic under Celine's flat, incurious gaze. She judged the housekeeper to be in her mid-fifties. She was tall, and sturdily built. The gray hair lay across a high smooth forehead, and there were deep lines between her brows and at the corners of her mouth.

Those eyes, Heather thought, flushing slightly as she gazed around the room, *are absolutely unreadable*. She was ashamed of herself for being unnerved—but there it was. The old house, once so friendly and filled with warmth, had changed for Heather. There was a quickening sense of something indefinably wrong, something that almost physically rejected her. The rooms she'd passed were dark.

But it's nonsense—your imagination, an inner

voice told Heather. *You're tired. And everything's bound to seem strange with Aunt Rachel gone.* With an effort she turned back to the woman.

"I really would like something to eat, if you don't mind," Heather said, and she knew her voice sounded tight and unnatural. "That is, if it's not too much trouble," she added hastily.

"I don't mind. But the food will be plain," the woman replied in her toneless voice. "I expect you're used to fancy things, back in America."

"Anything you'd like to make will be fine, really."

"It will take a short time to prepare." The woman spoke without apology.

"That's fine. I'll just go and get settled. I'd like to freshen up."

"There's no hot water. The heater is broken." Again, it was a flat statement. But something flickered in the polished, dark eyes.

Heather's self-confidence waned further. Why was the woman doing everything in her power to make her feel unwelcome? Surely it was not too much to expect friendlier treatment. This was her own house, she reminded herself, and Celine was a servant.

"I'll have the heater fixed," she said firmly. "But in the meantime, perhaps you'd be good enough to heat me a kettle of water to wash with."

The steady gaze flickered again, ever so slightly. "Yes, miss." Her mouth became a thin tight line, and she carried both suitcases from the room. Heather stood for a moment, feeling uncertain. She heard the housekeeper start up the staircase; there was nothing to do but follow her.

The staircase was steep and difficult to negotiate. The carpet that had once graced the stairs was gone now and all that remained were the tacks that had held it in place. The old bannister, suppported by carvings of fierce-looking dragons, was still very much intact and Heather found herself gripping it tightly as she ascended.

Ahead of her, Celine carried the bags along the wide shadowy corridor.

"Why all this dimness?" Heather asked. She reached out in passing and flicked on the overhead lights. If the woman was startled, she gave no sign, but strode steadily and silently toward Aunt Rachel's room.

Heather would have preferred to stay in the room she'd occupied as a child, but she couldn't summon the courage to tell Celine this. That would seem as if she were wavering—and heaven only knew what opinion of her this woman had already formed.

She stood in the doorway for a moment, unsure if she would ever feel comfortable. The large, heavy antique furniture was gloomy in the light of the lamp Celine had switched on. Ghostly associations with Aunt Rachel were everywhere—in the musty flowers of the old spread on the four-poster, and the ornate silver dresser set with its combs and mirrors and crystal jars for cream. Even the huge armoire with its ornate, time-blackened carving reminded her of Aunt Rachel. Here her aunt had allowed Heather to play hide-and-seek with imaginary playmates; Heather had stowed herself inside the old armoire, among the scented crepe, silk and jersey dresses that hung there. . . .

Heather shook off the mood of sad nostalgia. She must not give in to this sort of thing—this brooding over the unrecoverable past with all its memories.

Celine had set down the suitcases, and set about in a measured way, adjusting draperies, moving ornaments. "The room needs airing," she said. "I'm going to get the kettle." And without glancing at Heather she disappeared into the corridor.

Heather tried to make herself comfortable. She plumped a few cushions, then flung open the casement windows. She wouuldn't allow Celine's strange manner to upset her. The woman had had things pretty much to herself for six months. She had never met Heather and doubtless considered her an intruder. She would warm up in time, when she saw that Heather was not the kind of person to make all sorts of demands.

She breathed deeply, taking in the night air that was laden with soft, flowered scents from the vineyards and pastures of the valley. She heard a dim hum of voices from the tavern across the lane. It was a jolly place, especially on a Saturday night. Perhaps she would stop in now and then for a glass of the famous local wine.

Suddenly Heather gave an instinctive start. She had felt a presence beside her and whirled to face Celine.

"I've taken your kettle into the bathroom along the hall," said the housekeeper, her face and voice expressionless.

Heather willed her heart to stop pounding. She didn't wish Celine to know how startled she'd been—or how frightened. But anyone would react to being slipped up to so silently from behind, she told herself. And again she fumbled for words. "Yes, yes—thank you."

She fled the room aware of the eyes that followed her, and closed herself in the safety of the bathroom. Gratefully, she poured hot water into the flowered porcelain basin, ran a little cold in, and sponged her face. In the tarnished and steamy old mirror, her triangular face seemed to float, staring back at her with very large, very green eyes. Her skin seemed whiter than usual, and the small dusting of freckles on her nose and cheeks stood out more clearly in contrast.

Oh, dear, she thought. *I do look like a cat.* Frederic had teased her constantly about this, calling her his little kitten.

All at once her throat felt dry: the bitter memories flooded back, impossible to stop. *Frederic.* So tall, slender, athletic. He was like a sun-god, with his golden tan and dazzling smile. Almost every woman he met was completely smitten by him.

And in her heart Heather could not blame them. Nor could she blame Frederic, now that he was gone, for smiling at all of them, just as he had done at her that first day on the ski slopes above Zermatt.

But he had chosen her! They would have been married by now . . . just as soon as he had wound up a deal he was arranging for the sale of pictures from a famous estate. But all that had ended on that cruel day last April. They had argued; Frederic drove off in a huff. In his anger he hadn't seen the huge tractor trailer bearing down, ready to crush the little sports car.

Heather couldn't bear to think about the accident. Nor could she get over her sense of guilt: *she* had upset him—upset him so that he drove blindly, in a rage, straight to his cruel death.

Deliberately she splashed her face with cold water. She must fight off these wrenching memories and revive her flagging spirits. Celine had been little help, she thought ruefully, rubbing her face vigorously with the towel. Had she made a mistake in coming here? Her hopes that this house would be a haven, a place to heal her grief, seemed dashed. She could never recapture the happiness of the past. She had nothing to look forward to but a bleak present, a forbidding future.

You're letting it get the better of you, said that stern inner voice.

It started even before I got here—with that cruel-looking man I nearly ran over, Heather thought. And Celine's "welcome" certainly hadn't been encouraging.

Heather stood very straight. It was time to pull herself together. She would go downstairs to eat something and then try to relax. She left the sanctuary of the marble bathroom and went down to the dining room.

In a cold, forbidding silence, Celine proceeded to serve a simple but well-prepared meal. Despite her efforts to ignore the woman's obvious hostility Heather felt distinctly chilled.

She ate as quickly as possible, feeling a little absurd here in the dining room with its lovely Provencal furniture. Celine had disappeared, however, and Heather made her way back to the bedroom without seeing the housekeeper again.

From the casement window Heather could see a full moon beginning to rise, transforming the town and the countryside beyond. She sighed deeply; it was devastating to have no one with whom to share this beauty.

Dejectedly she crept into bed and buried herself deep in the protection of the fine spun sheets and fluffy comforter. She didn't expect to sleep easily or well; but soon, exhausted by her trip, she began to drift off.

Her dreams expressed a turmoil of emotions: painful images of Frederic, of Aunt Rachel, seemed to whirl sickeningly in her head. And there was a forbidding, malevolent presence somewhere among these . . . . Celine!

Abruptly, Heather sat bolt upright. She was very much awake, and as alert as a forest animal.

Those strange noises: what had they been?

She listened, straining every nerve. The noises had sounded far away and yet very close. Were they part of her dream?

Had they been footsteps? Whispers? Or perhaps the muffled small movements of some animal?

But there was only a still and breathless silence in the old house. The fantasy countours of Aunt Rachel's furniture gleamed in the light of the waning moon. The bed curtains were still; the mirrors seemed watery—pale, like silent pools.

Heather was sure her dreams had manufactured the noises. She felt as if she was floating between dream and reality. *If I pinch myself I'll wake up,* she thought.

She brushed away the hair that had fallen across her eyes. The touch of hand to forehead felt real enough.

Then she reached out and turned on her beside lamp. In its pale yellow glow the room seemed hardly less strange. Shadows loomed in the corners. The ancient wardrobe, stretching along almost the entire wall, seemed cloaked in secrets.

Heather drew the comforter around her and lay back. She tried to calm herself. There was nothing to fear—only memories had disturbed her dreams. She breathed deeply. She was behaving like a child, making nightmares out of common old things—bed curtains, gothic carvings, everyday furniture. The noises had been the product of her own mind—a mind over wrought by the events of the past few weeks.

She forced herself to think of pleasant things—of the high valleys she would roam, of the summer garden she would tend.

Gradually, in the ocher lamplight, the room became friendly and familiar. Heather's eyelids grew heavy, and again she slept.

Chapter 2

When Heather awoke, the sun was streaming through the curtains. From the valley, the fresh fragrance of meadow-sweet trees drifted into the room. The shadows of last night were emphatically gone.

Eagerly she clambered out of bed. Today would be the first day of her new life in Sion. Yesterday, with its gloomy portents and the strangeness of her meeting with Celine, would not count. She felt refreshed, almost elated. The dreams of her second sleep must have been good ones.

Another fragrance blended enticingly with the country smells of morning. Fresh coffee was brewing downstairs! It was a reassuring omen. Heather hurried to the bathroom to wash. The cold water was exhilarating, but a bit of a shock. She would have to do something about getting the heater fixed.

She dressed in clean jeans and a jersey, and slipped on a pair of comfortable shoes. Today would be a day of walking, of stretching her legs after all that driving. She would stroll around town and renew her acquaintance with the marketplace and the landmarks.

She skipped lightly down the staircase. It creaked agonizingly even under her slight weight. It really was in a poor state of repair! And those carpet tacks sticking up everywhere . . . she would take an inventory of things that needed doing, she decided. Celine had kept the house immaculately clean, of course, but she couldn't be expected to do much about things like this.

The housekeeper stood at the kitchen table, buttering toast. "Did you sleep well, miss?" she asked. She didn't exactly smile, but her severe clothing and precise movements seemed less forbidding here in the sun-bathed kitchen.

Heather resolved to win the woman over. "Yes, I did. It was like being a child again, in that big old bed," she replied with enthusiasm. Celine was not the sort of person with whom you talked about nightmares!

Celine's aloof demeanor did not change. "I've made coffee, and here's the toast. Will you have anything else?"

Heather settled into a chair, comforted by the sunlight as it glinted off the burnished copper utensils hanging on the walls; by the geraniums in the windows—even by the touch of the warm wooden tabletop. "Toast is fine, thank you." Gratefuly, she sipped at the aromatic café au lait that Celine had set before her. Her mind was filled with plans for the day. "Celine, where could I find a man to fix the hot-water heater?" she asked suddenly.

Celine raised her brows ever so slightly. It was the nearest she had come to any sign of animation. "Why there's always Peter Margaillou, I suppose." She shrugged her shoulders. "But . . . ."

"But what?"

"Well, that kind of work doesn't really interest him." Celine spoke as though she herself had not the remotest interest in the problem of the water heater.

Heather fought her impatience. "We've got to get it fixed, you know. How can you do the dishes? The laundry?"

"I've managed," Celine replied.

"Well, I hate to seem like a spoiled city girl—but I don't see how *I* can manage. . . ."

"Of course," said Celine, her eyes veiled. Heather noticed that those eyes held a strange yellowish light, a gleam that reminded her of something feral . . . a forest creature, perhaps, tense and watching. She shook off the thought.

"Wait," she announced. "I've just remembered someone. Old Oscar who used to do things for my great-aunt."

"Oscar Caron?" Celine's voice was dry as an autumn leaf.

"Yes, that's him."

"He doesn't come here anymore."

"But why ever not? He knew Aunt Rachel really well. They were friends."

"He hasn't been around for a long time," the housekeeper said stubbornly.

"Probably not. Not since Aunt Rachel died, anyway. Or was it before that?"

"It was . . . quite a while ago. Yes, before she died."

Heather sat back and stared at the housekeeper. The woman returned her look, but her mouth was rigid.

"I'd have thought," Heather said slowly, "that he would have come to visit her, especially when she was ill."

"Few people did," said Celine. Something seemed to move, to twist, deep in those lidded eyes.

Heather felt a rush of anger. "I suppose, Madame Dumas, you are referring to her family?"

The housekeeper did not reply.

Heather thought quickly. So that was why Celine seemed to resent her! She was naturally loyal to Aunt Rachel, and couldn't understand why a relative hadn't come to Sion when the old lady was dying—why the funeral and burial had been entrusted to lawyers.

"I see," she said. "I'll try to explain. You see, Rachel was father's aunt. And he died five years ago, leaving mother and I as her only American relatives . . . ."

"There's no need for you to explain," said Celine, turning away.

"But I want to! We've felt uncomfortable about the whole thing. We knew nothing of her illness. She hadn't written for the longest time. The last time I saw her was during a skiing vacation I took two years ago . . . before you came. She was fine, then. A little frail, but stubborn. She wouldn't come back to America. She wanted to stay here, in the house she'd shared with her husband, Maurice. She had another housekeeper then, who seemed a good competent woman."

Celine remained very still, her back rigidly turned to Heather. Was she listening at all? Heather plunged on.

"We did wonder, after a time, why her letters were so few and far between. We knew she'd changed housekeepers. She wrote us about you, told us how capable you were . . . ."

Celine did not budge.

"And I was busy at college. I'd become engaged

to Frederic, a young man I met here in Switzerland on that skiing trip. He . . . he traveled a lot, from Paris to New York, so I was able to see him." Heather made an effort to keep her voice steady. "I was going to come to Europe with him. Part of that trip was meant to be a visit to Aunt Rachel. To see about her health."

Celine pivoted to stare at Heather. The look was unreadable—not an accusation, but something else. Plain curiosity?

Heather went on. "But about seven months ago, mother became very ill. The trip was canceled. I dropped out of college for a while, to look after her. We haven't a great deal of money. Anyway, Frederic said he would find time to look in on Aunt Rachel. He had several trips to make, one of them to Geneva. It would be a simple thing to stop at Sion. Only a month or so passed. Frederic was in touch with mother and myself, to say he would be in Sion in a few days."

Heather drew a deep breath. Celine's eyes were on her, still and undecipherable.

"And then," Heather said, her own voice strange in her ears, "we got the telegram. Aunt Rachel was dead. Her husband's relatives would take care of things. We were terribly upset, but I couldn't leave mother just then. So it seemed the best thing—the only thing." Heather paused.

"I suppose Maurice's family cared very little when this house was willed to me. They have a lot of interests in Zurich. They were very comforting; Aunt Rachel had had the best care possible. They handled everything, like efficient Swiss. They even arranged to keep you here, until something could be done about the house."

Celine nodded.

Heather continued slowly, remembering those days. "When mother got well, six weeks, ago, I set out for Switzerland. I went to Paris to join Frederic. We were to be married, to come here together. . . ."

"To live here in Sion?" Celine asked. She seemed, for the first time, to respond to Heather's story.

"Maybe. Frederic was an art dealer. Switzerland is in the center of Europe, the center of everything as far as art dealers are concerned. Frederic joked about fixing up the old place—his work would have been easier, he said, if he could get away to a haven like this now and then. We were going to see how it worked out. . . ." Heather faltered, and her voice caught.

Celine watched silently.

"But then he was killed in a car accident. Frederic is dead." Heather's mind, even now, rebelled at this cruel reality. Tears welled in her eyes but she forced them back. "I ran back home to mother then. I couldn't face life without him, and I couldn't come here." Her voice was dull with the painful recollections. "So I hid from the world.

"But I decided it couldn't last. I knew Sion was the place. In a way, it's really the home of my childhood. I came to settle things up. And perhaps to stay." She looked directly at Celine now her chin rigid in defiance. "I *do* mean to stay, at least for a while."

There was a moment of leaden silence. Then Celine spoke. "Of course. It is your house."

The housekeeper busied herself with tidying the kitchen. Obviously, as far as she was concerned, the interview was over. If she was warmed by anything Heather had said, if she was placated— if she understood any of it at all—she gave no sign.

Heather slumped unhappily for a moment watching her. Perhaps Celine was permanently cold, unyielding. She shivered at a sudden thought: poor Aunt Rachel, alone with this rigid automaton during her last lonely days!

Heather gave an audible sigh and pushed her chair away from the table. "I'm going downtown. I'll find Oscar, and ask him to come along and fix a few things around here."

Celine didn't reply, and Heather could feel those strange eyes watching her as she left the room.

Now as she walked quickly into town, she remembered that Oscar Caron lived over an old shop on Haute Street. It was a narrow, twisting and cobbled thoroughfare, not much more than a laneway. In the window boxes belonging to buildings of indeterminable age, brave summer flowers sought the meager sunlight that filtered through. The windows of the shops had tiny lead-edged panes, and small guild signs hung over the doorways. It was just like a picture postcard, as quaint as any American's dream of old Europe, Heather thought to herself.

She hoped Oscar would remember her. She had known him in the early days, when father's fortunes were high, and the Ashleys had visited Aunt Rachel nearly every summer. She would have been about twelve years old when she saw him last. It was a startling thought, here in the old street that hadn't changed substantially for hundreds of years. . . .

Here it was! Number eighty-four. As always, Oscar's small wooden dollhouses were displayed in the windows. The oak door was scarred and creaky, and a bell tinkled as she opened it. The shop was exactly the same as it had been ten years ago. Heather felt as though she had taken a magical step backward in time.

A white head was bending over some minute task at a table near the rear of the shop. The man looked up. The thatch of hair was as unruly as ever, the blue eyes undimmed, the mustache crisply turned and waxed. It *was* Oscar.

"Can I help you?" he asked. The voice was rumbling and kind, obviously he did not recognize her.

"Oscar—Mr. Caron . . . I'm Heather Ashley. Do you remember me?"

He rose, brushing bits of wood from his fingers. He squinted at her elaborately, and cocked his head to one side.

He's old, thought Heather with a sharp pang. *He doesn't remember me after all.* In her confusion she was unable to meet his gaze. She blushed, and looked awkwardly around the shop.

In the dim and crowded space, she hadn't noticed that someone else was watching her. She started a little as her eyes met his: the cool gray gaze was oddly familiar. It was the man she'd nearly run over yesterday.

He stood very tall, lean and square, not four feet away. He looked as though she had interrupted him, his expression faintly contemptuous.

Heather flushed more deeply. It seemed she would never stop feeling clumsy and strange. A memory of Celine's implacable gaze rose clearly in her mind. She had an urge to turn and flee, to escape that powerful scrutiny.

But Oscar came to her rescue.

"Why it *is*—it's young Miss Ashley," he said with a slow smile.

Heather turned gratefully back to him. He held

out one large and gnarled hand to be shaken, and she clasped it in both of hers.

"Oscar, I'm so glad you remember me. I haven't seen you in years."

"Not since you were a child—you're hardly a little girl these days. So grown-up—and pretty, too!"

"I'm here to take care of things—about Aunt Rachel's house and all . . . she left it to me, you see. . . ."

"Is that a fact? Rachel Savorin. . . ." Oscar's faded blue eyes turned misty for a moment. "I remember her well, you know. But I'm afraid I hadn't seen her much this past year or so. She got a little funny, I guess, the way we old people do." He rubbed his mustache thoughtfully. "Perhaps it had to do with that housekeeper, the Dumas woman. She's nothing like your aunt was, you know. Now Rachel, she was a good woman. Everyone knew her husband, respected him; Maurice was a smart fellow, excellent businessman.

"But along comes Celine Dumas, not so very long ago. Never talks to anyone—fixes you with that cold eye. . . ."

Heather, glad she was not alone in her reaction to Celine, could not suppress a nervous laugh.

The tall man, whose presence she'd been trying to ignore, spoke up unexpectedly.

"The woman's completely efficient. I, for one, never had cause to quarrel with her." His voice was deep and strong.

Oscar gave a hearty snort. "Perhaps not, my friend. But many others have. Most of Rachel Savorin's oldest friends were made to feel unwelcome in her house. Maybe because you didn't fall into that category. . . ." Oscar caught himself suddenly, and turned to Heather. "But I have been terribly rude! Miss Ashley, may I introduce to you Dr. Valdemar?"

Heather turned to the tall man, trying her best to look gracious and serene. "I suppose," she said lightly, "in a manner of speaking, we *have* met."

The doctor's deeply tanned face remained impassive. His hair was very dark, and under the rugged brow his gray eyes seemed cold as a pale sky in autumn. He shrugged a little.

Did he even associate her with the little incident yesterday, Heather wondered, feeling foolish once more.

But the doctor spoke politely enough, saying, "How do you do? I'm sorry, but I don't remember when we met."

Why had she mentioned their encounter? He *hadn't* remembered, but now she would have to explain. No doubt she would be exposed to his anger and scorn all over again! She forced lightness into her voice. "I nearly ran into you on the street yesterday."

"On the street? So it was you in that gray sports car?"

"Yes." Heather's chin was uptilted. He could say whatever he liked, but it had been entirely accidental, and no harm had been done. If he wished to berate her . . . .

But he didn't. Instead he spoke of Aunt Rachel. "I knew your aunt just slightly, having been her physician for only a few months. I took over old Dr. Mazarell's practice for a while when he was ill. I did as much as was possible for her. She seemed—well, stubborn and reclusive."

"But that was so unlike her!" exclaimed Heather.

"Perhaps. But elderly people sometimes do

strange things, Miss Ashley." His voice was firm. He turned to examine something on a shelf.

Heather was puzzled. She was being dismissed again. But perhaps they all assumed that the death of an old lady—a woman whose family had left her alone in her final days—was of no consequence.

Oscar rumbled on about Celine. "She's from some other canton, you know. Vaud or the Grisons, I forget which. Turned up here suddenly, a year or more ago, and took over things at your aunt's house. It wasn't the same after that. I'd have been more than glad to keep fixing things for Rachel Savorin if Celine hadn't made it so difficult. . . ." He shook his white-thatched head.

"Do you mean Celine kept you away?" Heather asked.

Oscar looked at her, his gaze very level. After a moment he spoke. "She said I wasn't welcome."

There was such ruffled dignity in his bearing that Heather smiled. "Oh, Oscar—if I'd had anything to do with it, if I'd been there . . . ." She felt a tiny stab of remembered guilt. She *hadn't* been there. No one had. No one had protected Aunt Rachel from that woman.

There was a slight impatient movement from Dr. Valdemar. Oscar brightened suddenly. "Oh, but we are keeping the good doctor waiting! Let me just settle up this little transaction. Then we'll talk."

Heather gave the doctor a look of distracted apology and wandered toward the shelves that filled the little store. Lightly she touched the wooden toys that stocked them, a jumble of wooden animals, little cars, dolls, miniature furniture—all lovingly made by hand in Oscar's workshop. He had been fashioning these marvelously detailed toys for several years, and had become something of a local legend. Heather had warm memories of the wondrous hours she'd spent with a very special Noah's ark made of wood and filled with a small carved Noah, Mrs. Noah, and brightly colored animals, all in pairs. As a child, Heather had often played alone—and the fantasies and dreams she'd spun with the ark were still vivid in her mind.

The familiarity of this scaled-down world of children's toys served to calm Heather. The talk about Celine and Aunt Rachel had been unsettling. And Dr. Valdemar had certainly disturbed her. She was keenly aware of him, of how close he seemed, here in the confines of the little shop. She could hear him discussing with Oscar the merits of a certain toy.

At length, the sale was completed. Heather, wandering dreamily among grinning marionettes, music boxes and Swiss clocks, heard the cash register ring. She saw Oscar begin to box and wrap the doctor's purchase. With a little start of recognition she saw that the toy was a Noah's ark, very similar to the one she'd had as a child.

How strange—just when she'd been thinking about her own ark. But she knew Oscar was rather well-known for this special toy. Many were exported to other countries, and she'd even seen them in shops in Boston—not to mention Paris.

With a nod Dr. Valdemar ducked out of the store, his package under his arm.

"Now," said Oscar, "we can talk!"

Heather spoke hurriedly. "I don't want to keep you from your work. I really came because I don't know who to ask, and—well, the water heater in my house isn't working. Celine doesn't seem to know anyone who can fix it."

"I see." Oscar's eyes twinkled a little. "You remembered I used to do odd jobs for your Aunt Rachel. Well, as I've explained, I myself haven't set foot in that house for some time—and really, I can't do that kind of work anyway. But I'll see who comes to mind. . . . I don't mind telling you, that Dumas woman isn't popular in this town. Not many would work for her. But for *you* . . . wait, I know. There's a fellow I know . . . he's reliable. . . . Wait." Oscar pottered off to a back room where there was a telephone.

So, Celine was going to be quite a problem then. Heather shuddered inwardly at the thought of having to deal with her. She mustn't let the woman gain the upper hand. And yet so far Celine had managed to do just that.

Oscar returned, smiling benevolently. "Now don't you worry about a thing, my girl. He'll drop over today."

"Oscar, you're a lifesaver! But I feel terrible that you don't want to come to the house yourself. . . . Not about the work, of course, but because of Celine's caused trouble."

"Never mind. Rachel was old, but you're a modern young lady. You can handle Celine. But perhaps you aren't going to stay, and the problem will solve itself?" He eyed her from under bushy brows.

"I don't know, Oscar. I thought I might stay—I like it here. And eventually I could bring my mother over. . . ."

"I remember her, and your papa, too."

"Father died five years ago."

"I'm sorry—"

"Oh, no. We're over it now. It was rough at the time but . . . ." She did not need to tell Oscar about

Frederic. It would only reopen her own wounds. His stricken look at the news of her father's death had been enough. She hadn't been to see Oscar on her visit two years before when she'd met Frederic.

Oscar doubtlessly saw her as an extension of the happy child he'd known several years ago. He was an old man, and too many details of her life would only confuse him.

"Oscar, I'm going to fix it at the house so you can come and have tea. Just like the old days," Heather said warmly.

The old man smiled. "Thank you. I only hope Celine does not protest too much."

Heather felt much better. She was not entirely certain how to handle Celine, but the determination to do so was strong within her.

Then she wished him good day, explaining she must get back to the house, to prepare for the arrival of the repairman.

She hurried along the winding little street, rehearsing all the way the speech she would make to the hostile Celine. *Now look*, she'd begin. *This is my house now. I appreciate that you are an efficient housekeeper. But you must try to be more pleasant.* How lame it sounded! Heather walked faster, suddenly angry at being on the defensive this way. *I know—I'll threaten to fire her.* Could you fire someone because she refused to smile? Because people didn't like her? That would hardly be fair, Heather realized. But there was something more disturbing than that—something tugging at the back of her mind. Suddenly she stood stock-still, staring into space.

Something was very wrong in the fact that Celine seemed to have deliberately shut Aunt Rachel off from everyone else. And her "efficiency"? That had been confirmed by the doctor—Dr. Valdemar—who was himself a rather strange, saturnine figure.

She renewed her brisk stride, hastily cutting through the streets of the old town. Her head was so filled with the various dimensions of her problem that she hardly noticed her surroundings. The potted flowers and shop signs all sped by in a blur of color.

She rounded the corner of the inn and collided solidly with someone going the other way.

"Hey, watch were you're going, can't you?" exclaimed a male voice.

Heather's bottled-up anger suddenly flared. "Why don't *you* watch where *you're* going?"

A young man, with very blue eyes and a shock of sandy hair, was grinning down at her. "I *was*," he said "but you came around that corner like a train from a tunnel."

"Well, I'm in a hurry," said Heather, still indignant.

"I can *see* that! But look what you've made me do!"

Heather eyed the front of his shirt. There on the pale broadcloth was a sticky stain. She traced its source to the ice-cream cone in his right hand.

"Oh, I am sorry," she apologized.

"But if I'd grow up and stop eating ice-cream cones, none of this would have happened. Right?" The young man dabbed at his shirt with a large, floppy handkerchief. "Well, you *are* right. If I hadn't been concentrating on Swiss chocolate mocha, I could have sidestepped and missed this delightful encounter altogether."

His accent was lightly Scottish, Heather decided. He looked rather comical, juggling the dripping cone and the handkerchief. All the while his eyes fixed eagerly on her face.

Then his smile broadened even more. "But I have an idea. We can settle out of court if you'll let me buy *you* an ice-cream cone."

"I really don't have time. Honestly. But thanks." She couldn't help returning his smile as she started to walk away.

He looked stricken. "You just can't do this! Please—now that we've met and all—"

"But we haven't met."

"I'm Malcolm McBride. I'm a writer. There. Now you've met me. And you're the dark lady and your name is—"

"Heather."

"Heather. See? Now we've met. You can't get away. You're trapped."

Heather laughed. "We'll see about that." She turned and strode briskly on her way.

Malcolm stood on the sidewalk holding his ice-cream cone. "You won't get away, you know; I'll follow you to the ends of the earth!" he called after her. He didn't seem to care that passersby were giving him amused and tolerant looks.

Heather turned and waved. He had made her forget about Celine, and she smiled to herself nearly all the way home. It was the first time in weeks she had felt lighthearted enough to see beyond her personal tragedy. She felt a resurgence of hope that not even Celine's overt unfriendliness could quell.

Chapter 3

Heather entered the house, this time with her own key. The halls and rooms were polished and silent; the drapes drawn. Celine was nowhere to be found.

It was impossible not to recoil at the tomblike silence. Heather didn't remember the house being this gloomy when Aunt Rachel was alive. Windows would be opened wide then, letting the summer breezes billow the fragile curtains. Light streamed in joyfully. Flowers crowded every window, yielding delightful perfumes.

The first step was obvious. Heather busied herself at every window, throwing wide the heavy drapes and raising all the sashes. The window boxes were in a sorry condition. She dug into them with feverish energy. On Saturday she would go to the market and get boxes of geraniums, petunias— anything for color, to return the happiness to this house.

Her rush of energy unabated, Heather went to the garden. It was tangled and unkempt, sorely in need of a pair of loving hands. She set to work, ruthlessly pulling endless weeds; vines were trimmed, pinched and pruned. The leggy old rosebushes were savagely attacked, and made to climb in orderly fashion over their trellises. The jumbled, overgrown herb garden was set to rights.

Heather was elbow-deep in good soil, and a thin perspiration dampened her forehead. It was good to spend energy like this—not to waste it on fear and anger, or grief.

Heather sat on her heels for a moment, listening to the birds chatter and splash in their bath of moss-covered stone. She realized that she had spent these past few hours without thinking even once of Frederic. But now that she had thought of him again, the pain returned with double force.

Frederic. His lopsided grin, so casual yet urbane, seemed to taunt her.

Frederic had known all there was to know about the exciting world of art and antiques. He would have been a big success. There was no doubt in Heather's mind. He had already been well on his way, with lightning trips from one part of the world to another, attending glittering parties with Heather, who tried not to feel ill at ease. But she would learn, he said. It was all part of his work.

Heather still felt rather foolish remembering herself at those parties. She seemed always at a loss for something to say. And for the right thing to wear.

Frederic had insisted on supplying dresses, ignoring mother's Bostonian ideas of propriety. After all, they would soon be married, wouldn't they? And besides, Frederic only expected Heather to go to these gatherings now and then, if he happened to be in Boston or New York. She really must get used to them, they played an important role in his business.

Even if after their marriage they chose to live in Switzerland, they would probably travel a great deal—to London, Paris, Madrid, New York, Washington.

The life of the jet set, thought Heather. I wonder if I would ever have got used to it all? But how could she not with Frederic at her side, so handsome and dazzling . . . dazzling to her and to every other woman he met. *But how wretched I was to be jealous*, Heather thought, angry again with herself.

He had chosen her, after all, that first day they had met on the white alpine slopes.

He'd been delighted to learn that technically she was not American, but Swiss. "That's the one thing you can't buy in the world. A Swiss passport."

Heather had never thought about it before. She'd been born here, that time her parents came to Europe for a long stay. She'd thought of herself as both Swiss and American. And so she was. Well, it seemed to please Frederic, at any rate.

But she was no glamorous international traveler, despite all those transatlantic vacations during her childhood. She was a psychology student at Boston University; eventually she wanted to work with emotionally disturbed children.

The advent of Frederic had clarified her goals. She had wanted only one thing: Frederic. And the miracle was, *he* wanted *her*. She knew that, knew it through all the bouts of jealousy and insecurity.

Even that last time, that last terrible day when she'd spotted him having a cozy Parisian luncheon with Geraldine. . . .

The thought of Geraldine, however, still brought a bitter taste to her mouth. Geraldine, the glossy blonde, with swept-back hair, and sophisticated, flamboyant clothes. Geraldine, who made Heather feel awkward and too innocent when they had met a few times at those glamorous parties.

Frederic, accosted, at first denied anything but a business connection with Geraldine. He was soothing, generous with Heather in her unreasonable jealousy. But when she had weepily persisted he had lost his temper. He stomped out of the hotel, into the street and roared off in his car.

She never saw him again.

And all because she had behaved like a possessive child. Her heart gave a familiar wrench at the memory as guilt flooded through her.

Heather rose and picked up her tools. She walked slowly, aimlessly, in the general direction of the house. As she neared the back steps, a harsh voice broke into her thoughts. "The windows. What are they doing open?"

Heather looked up to see Celine, arms akimbo, standing in the doorway. Her eyes were fierce, and she was obviously annoyed.

Heather had no strength to argue. "Close them if you like," she said tonelessly.

Celine pursed her lips and disappeared.

Heather sat on the stoop, and sighed audibly.

"Hey!" called a masculine voice. Heather looked up. She could see no one. The stone wall around the garden was a high solid one. It was unlikely that anyone could be heard so clearly from the other side. She looked behind her, up at the house, and back and forth to each side. There was no one around.

"Hey!" came the voice again. Heather frowned. If this was someone's idea of a joke . . . .

She looked around again, then stood up and walked a short distance from the steps. She had the distinct but illogical impression that the voice had come from above.

"Do you live here?" the voice asked. It seemed nearer now. She looked in the direction of a great and very old oak tree, whose trunk rose from outside the wall. The branches swayed oddly and spread over part of the wall and garden. Heather walked over. Looking up she could see the soles of a pair of rather large shoes jutting out from a branch, and above that, among the shifting leaves, a grinning face topped with a shock of sandy hair. . . .

"Yes, I live here," said Heather. "What do you think you're doing?"

"I told you I'd follow you to the ends of the earth. . . ."

"This is not the ends of the earth. This is private property."

"Come on now, be kind. I climbed all the way up here after all." Malcolm gave her a look of desperate appeal.

"Just to spy on me, you did that?"

"No. Not really. I did it to get a better look at the house—and that courtyard over there."

"We don't use that side of the house."

"I thought not. It's fascinating, isn't it? I'm very interested in old houses. Come on, let me come and visit you. It's strictly for purposes of research." Malcolm began to clamber noisily in the tree.

"Just don't fall and break your neck," laughed Heather. "I don't want you to sue me."

Swinging by his arms from a sturdy branch, Malcolm looked shocked. "How could I do a thing like *that*?" He dropped to the ground with a surprising lightness. "See? Here I am, your hero. I saw you there, you know, looking all sad and desolate. I had to come to your rescue."

Heather was a little disconcerted. "I'm all right."

It was an odd feeling to know that Malcolm had

been watching her that way. But she had an instinctive trust in the owner of those clear blue eyes and that open grin. She strolled along the garden pathway. "Now tell me about this 'research' you're doing," she said. Malcolm shambled eagerly along beside her.

"Well, I told you I'm a writer. I write mystery stories. I write utterly horrible potboilers with lots of atmosphere. And I make a good living doing it."

Heather smiled. "Sounds like fun."

"Well, it's a living. Actually, I'm a serious fellow. I have a deep and abiding urge to make my mark in some respectable way. So I'm digging into local history. I want to do a weighty tome about Sion."

"It's a very old town," commented Heather.

"Yes," agreed Malcolm, growing more enthusiastic. "People have been tramping up this valley since Roman times and before. In fact the whole story of Switzerland is a fantastic old hodgepodge. I settled on this town because it's quaint, what with the bishop's palaces and all. It's not so frequented by tourists that the old buildings are completely lost by way of being 'restored'.

"And it's got houses like this one," he added. "No, really. That older part could be hundreds of years old," he continued as Heather waved a deprecating hand at him. "I'd really like to take a good look at it. It *may* be important."

"It's just an old dump," laughed Heather.

"Maybe not. I'm going to get my hands on a few old maps and plans. Check the public library and church archives." He paused. "Anyway, it's really important to me to do something *serious*. Those mystery thrillers are an embarrassment. I can't even tell my friends I write the things—"

"What nonsense. You should be glad you've got *that* much creativity. Most of us don't."

"You're a nice girl, Heather. I knew you were the first time you squashed ice cream into my shirt."

Heather laughed again. Malcolm stood still and stared at her for a long moment, his eyes suddenly cloudy.

"Say, what was it that made you so sad, just then?"

Silent for a moment, Heather plucked at an errant shrub. Then she spoke in a low voice. "Oh, Malcolm, please don't. I don't want to talk about it. I . . . I don't even know you. I wouldn't ordinarily have admitted there *was* anything sad on my mind. You found out by spying, so I don't have to tell you."

He sighed. "All right. I'll behave. But who was that lady at the door—that somewhat stern creature?" he asked, following her as she walked along the grassy path.

"That's Celine; she's the housekeeper here. You see, I only arrived last night. This house belonged to my great-aunt. She died some months ago. For various reasons I've only just now come to live here. Celine was my aunt's housekeeper, and she stayed on. I hardly know her myself."

"I hate to say this, but she reminds me of my landlady—a deadly harridan if there ever was one."

"Well," said Heather rather hesitantly, "she hasn't been overly pleasant to me, I must admit. She isn't exactly mean—just cold as stone. I found myself wondering if I'd done the right thing to come here at all."

"Perhaps it's natural that she should resent you," he commented, nodding thoughtfully. "She had the house all to herself before you got here, didn't she?"

"Yes, I guess she did."

"Well, then, now you've come along to take over, and probably she thinks you're going to upset her orderly little life here. Right?"

"That's possible. I certainly hope that's all there is to it."

"Aha!" cried Malcolm, stopping short and hunching his shoulders comically. "A mystery is it then?"

"Don't be silly. Not *exactly* a mystery, anyway. But why would she—" Heather stopped short. She felt she was saying too much, even to this obviously friendly listener. There was no logical basis for the odd thoughts that were circling her mind.

"Why would she what?" asked Malcolm eagerly.

"Nothing. Nothing at all," Heather replied firmly. "I suppose she just doesn't like me, that's all. Maybe I'm a foreigner to her."

"Look, I'm sorry if it seemed that I was spying. I wasn't really. I got up in that tree, and I saw you sitting there looking sad and—I was really sort of ashamed of my little joke. I knew you lived here—"

"How?"

"I asked around. I wanted to see the house, and look over the courtyard wall. And I was kind of hoping I'd see you. But there you were, and I really didn't want to intrude—luckily the dragon lady interrupted you first."

"You're forgiven," Heather announced. She checked her watch. "Look at that! Four o'clock. I'm famished. I wonder if Celine would let us root around in her kitchen. . . ."

"What a superb idea!" said Malcolm enthusiastically.

"That way you can have a look at the house," Heather said.

"And protect you from Celine," added Malcolm.

"I don't *need* protection in my own house." Heather's voice was firm. "And I don't want to talk about it anymore. She's just a housekeeper. That's *all*."

"Come along, then," said Malcolm, offering his arm.

Celine was reserved, but not outwardly upset by Malcolm's visit. She was, in fact, in the process of preparing supper, and in her distant mechanical way, set before them an ample meal. Smacking his lips over potted paté and fresh white bread, Malcolm whispered that perhaps Heather should forget about Celine's manners, in view of her excellent skills as a cook.

Heather couldn't suppress a conspiratorial chuckle. "I told you to stop that," she whispered fiercely. "Let's talk about something else. Like yourself, for example. Why would you come all the way to Switzerland to look at old houses? Surely there are plenty of those in Scotland?"

"So you guessed where I'm from," laughed Malcolm, exaggerating his burr. "Well, to tell you the truth, I happen to *like* it here, better than Scotland. Switzerland has a different sort of history . . . infinitely more fascinating. Say, this is a rather fine wine."

"It's from our own cellars. Aunt Rachel's husband was a wine merchant."

"Eureka! I've found the perfect girl!" Malcolm crowed, slapping the table.

"Far from it," said Heather, pushing her chair back. "Let's take our little tour of this place."

Heather paused to explain their mission to Celine, who merely nodded impassively. "By the way, did anyone come about the water heater?" she asked, suddenly remembering.

"No, miss," replied Celine. "But I've been out much of the day."

"Oh, well. Maybe he'll come tomorrow," Heather said.

She and Malcolm began a long trek through the house, exploring every room in the new section, while Malcolm exclaimed over details of the wainscoting, the paneling, the fine old door and window fixtures. He seemed to admire it all immensely, especially the massive oak armoire in the room Heather now occupied. He knew a good deal about the architecture, pointing out aspects Heather had hardly noticed before.

But he was particularly interested in the older part of the house, and asked Heather if he might see that, too.

"Oh, we can't go inside," Heather told him. "It's boarded up—and it'll be dark soon. There are no lights; it could be dangerous. I explored it once when I was little. It's all dust and bat droppings."

"But that makes it more interesting," persisted Malcolm.

"Well, we'll have to go another time," Heather sighed. "Though I can't imagine what there is to interest you there. The place is empty."

"Just the same, I'd like to see it."

Heather gave him a bemused look. For now you'll have to forget it—I've had quite a day and feel in need of a hot bath, for which I shall have to boil innumerable kettles of water since the man hasn't come to fix the heater."

Malcolm gave her an expansive grin. "No problem," he declared. "I'll take a look at it. I expect you have us writers stereotyped as nothing but intellectuals. However, I am highly skilled at practical stuff like that. Lead the way, please."

The heater reposed in a dark corner of the cellar. It was an ancient thing, but with much muttering and calling for tools, Malcolm managed to get it working again.

"Don't pay me," he announced. "Another supper like this evening's will do nicely. Here, let me have that flashlight."

Heather handed it to him, and he shone it into the corners of the basement. The wine racks stood on one side, facing a blank wall. "I suppose that's the wall dividing the cellar and the old house," he said thoughtfully.

"It's on that side, of course. But there's no cellar there."

"There isn't?"

"No. It's deceptive, but only the more recent part of this house has a cellar. It slopes down from the original structure, which was built on flat land. So what you're seeing is a wall shared with the *main* level of the old house. Directly across from us, through that wall, there's only a stone floor."

"Really?" said Malcolm. "Now that's interesting."

"Come on, let's get out of all this mold and dust."

They emerged from the cellar thoroughly grimy and Heather hoped there would soon be enough hot water to take a bath.

Malcolm seemed to read her mind, saying, "All right, milady, your bath will be ready to draw shortly." He made a little bow, and added, "I'll be off now, and leave you to it. I must say, today has been—an extreme pleasure."

"Thank you for fixing the heater," Heather

said, a little embarrassed by his bright eager gaze.

Malcolm grinned, and with a flourish he shook her hand. Encountering Celine in the hallway as he went toward the front door, he gave her a little bow, too, and wished her a very polite good evening.

Celine's frosty stare refused to melt.

Much later, after a long and fragrant soak in the tub, Heather curled into her pillows, sleepily scanning a book. But her eyes were too heavy to read and she snapped off the light. She drifted almost immediately into deep sleep. . . .

There were small muffled sounds, odd sounds, voices far away. They were calling her. She knew them, but they drifted away again, becoming furtive . . . they scraped and scratched and murmured and thumped.

Heather opened her eyes. The room was silent; everything appeared to be exactly the same. But this time she knew she had heard them again; the noises were not part of her dreams. She looked at the luminous dial of her watch. It was very late, almost 3:00 A.M. She shivered, and drew the bedclothes closer.

Had she really heard anything? She felt so strange. Had she heard the same noises as last night, or just sounds in her head? It was possible that her imagination was playing tricks, manufacturing those noises to justify the irrational fear she had felt last night. . . .

Then she heard it unmistakably.

And this time she was wide awake.

Chapter 4

In the silence that followed, the beating of her own heart seemed thunderous in her ears. But she strained for that *other* sound. She would know it if it came.

She heard it again. Something muffled—something hollow? Scratchings? Footsteps—muffled and far?

Heather felt her scalp begin to tingle. Carefully, she drew herself up into a sitting position. The noises continued—ghostly, but real. Where were they coming from?

Slowly, Heather's eyes investigated the room—the fireplace, the dresser . . . . Inevitably her gaze was drawn to the giant armoire.

With cold certainty she knew that somehow those noises were coming from the armoire.

It loomed black in the moonlit room: an ancient, gnarled cabinet, filled with secrets.

Drawing a deep breath, Heather slipped out of bed. Her bare feet making no sound on the carpet as she made her way to the armoire.

She stood in front of it, her heart continuing to

beat wildly. She stretched out a shaky hand and touched the key: it was there; she had only to turn it.

The noises continued. They seemed louder now—louder, but still muffled.

Stories from Heather's childhood crowded into her head: for some reason, the six dead wives of Bluebeard leaped into her mind. Would she find them inside, all pale and ghostly and spattered with blood, their hair in tangled confusion? And their voices murmuring, murmuring?

Heather made an effort to calm herself. *Don't be ridiculous*, she told herself. *You're only scaring yourself even more.* Deliberately, she reached for the key, and slowly, silently, turned it.

She was met with the scent of old lavender. She swung the armoire door very wide. Moonlight filtered in from the window. She could see the linen, piled neatly on shelves, and large black trunk sitting on the floor of the wardrobe. With trembling fingers, she fumbled at the clasps. They snapped sharply open.

Lifting the lid, she peered into the trunk. She could make out very little of its contents.

What am I doing? I need the light! Quickly Heather tiptoed back to the bed and switched on the lamp. She stood, still, listening. The noises had stopped.

The trunk was a very old-fashioned one, filled to the top with clothing. There was no question at all about those dresses—crepes, silks and jerseys, flower-printed and dignified. They had been Aunt Rachel's, the ones she'd stored for years in this wardrobe on hangers; Celine must have put them into the trunk.

Heather lifted a few out, exploring deeper in the trunk, but she found nothing else.

She began to feel foolish. What was the matter with her anyway? What had she expected to find? Then the noises began again.

Heather ran across the room and opened the door. The hall, lit only by the moonlight streaming in through one high narrow window, was dark and, as far as she could tell, totally deserted. Suddenly, she had the distinct impression that the house was empty, that there was no one there but herself. "Celine! Mrs. Dumas," she called out, shivering in her nightgown in the long dark corridor.

There was no answer. The house was completely quiet again. There wasn't a sound anywhere. It was almost as if it were waiting for something to happen. All the strange muffled noises had subsided now and she was alone, the deep dark silence all around her. "Celine," she cried again, this time more loudly. "Mrs. Dumas!"

There was no response, only the faint echo of her own voice. Celine must be somewhere in the house, she told herself. Why didn't she come? Where was she?

Horrified, she realized that Celine had left her all alone in a house that now seemed menacing and forbidding, alive with strange noises and lurking terrors in its shadowy corners. *There's no way I'm going to wander around in the dead of night trying to find out where she is*, she thought.

Heather suddenly realized she was very cold, and shivering violently, she turned and made her way back into her bedroom where she slipped back under the warm covers and pulled them up to her chin. She lay there for a long time, staring at the open wardrobe. The massive piece of furniture looked almost alive—hostile and malevolent. There was something about it that was sly, deceptive.

Heather had a feeling that its heavy wood doors guarded the key to some old secret.

Her thoughts turned from the armoire to Celine Dumas. Could she really have left the house without any explanation at all?

The minutes passed slowly. Heather's breathing returned to normal, and the nightmarish noises receded from her mind.

She fell into a restless sleep, the beside lamp still burning.

THE NEXT MORNING, Celine was at her usual post in the kitchen.

"Where were you last night?" Heather asked without preamble.

"Why I was here," she replied. "I was in my room. Why do you ask?"

Heather was impatient at the woman's calm exterior. She felt nervous and agitated as she replied, "Because I called you in the middle of the night, and you didn't answer. Were you out?"

"Of course not," said Celine, turning now to fix Heather with her hooded eyes. Heather began to feel a little foolish. She *had* been panicky last night, perhaps a little irrational.

Heather decided to throw all caution to the winds and tell Celine exactly what had happened. "It's just that I heard some very strange noises in the house last night. They woke me from a sound sleep. I was very frightened. I ran out of my bedroom into the hall and called for you, but you didn't answer."

"I'm a very heavy sleeper, miss," Celine replied quietly as she placed the sugar bowl on the table and poured milk and coffee into a cup. "Strange noises, you say?"

Heather nodded silently, fascinated with the

older woman's eyes. There was no flicker of emotion in them. Only that odd, yellowish glow.

"Your room is right next to the wall of the old unused part of the house," said Celine. "You probably heard rats scurrying around in there."

Then, with a shadow of a smile on her thin lips, she added, "In such an old house as this, you have to get used to that kind of thing." For some reason, she seemed willing to talk now. "Take me, for instance," she continued. "My room is near that wall, too, but I'm used to hearing rats in the other house so I sleep very well at night."

She turned from the table and disappeared into the pantry where Heather heard the tinkle of glass. Then she returned and began tidying up some of the kitchen cupboards.

Heather finished her breakfast, thinking carefully. Then she turned to the older woman again, saying, "I'm going to visit the old house, Celine."

"I don't think you should. The doors and windows were boarded up a while ago. Besides, it's not really safe in there anymore. Mrs. Savorin knew that and took all the necessary precautions. Why do you want to go over there, anyway?"

"Oh, I just thought it would be fun. I used to spend a lot of time there when I was a child," she said, hoping Celine wouldn't question her reasons too deeply.

Celine said nothing further and proceeded to clear the table and put the dirty dishes in the sink. "Well, you can't go there, not anymore," she said finally. "When I first got here I went over to the old place. The staircase was unsafe. Only the mice and rats live there now. That's what you must have heard last night."

Heather was far from happy with that explanation. But for the moment she was willing to let the matter drop. Celine's rigid façade was unlikely to crack more than it had just done. Heather told herself to be grateful for the civil exchange, and for the information Celine had unwittingly given her.

It appeared that Celine was most anxious that Heather remain incurious about the noises, and about the old section of the house. And it would be prudent to let her think that the matter had been dropped.

Casually, Heather rose from the large old table. Inwardly, her mind was busy. She could go into the old house anytime she liked, of course, no matter what Celine said. But she would have to plan things carefully.

Something was going on. Heather sensed it instinctively. She wondered if that something had anything to do with Aunt Rachel's strange behavoir—her "reclusiveness," as Dr. Valdemar had called it.

Why hadn't she bothered to find out where Malcolm was staying? He would be her logical partner in any such exploration.

Well, Heather was certain, she would be hearing from Malcolm again soon. Meanwhile, there was still a lot she could do without his aid.

She was determined to thoroughly explore the wardrobe. She was certain it was the key to the noises, and their meaning.

Back in her bedroom, she eyed the gloomy old armoire as if it were a living, breathing enemy. It seemed to glower at her, to brood. Perhaps the mutterings were its own?

But the massive doors, the carved oaken gargoyles, were definitely inanimate. They could not *really* emanate negative forces. The wardrobe had been built with love, several years ago, by some kindhearted artisan.

By someone like Oscar, Heather thought, and this made her feel a little better.

Still, there seemed to be some dark message in those heavy doors. At any moment, they might swing open to reveal someone standing inside; or *something*, Heather thought, shuddering.

But common sense soon drove these malevolent fantasies from her mind. The wardrobe was filled with linen and old clothing. Perhaps, she thought, I should do something about those dresses—get them ready to be given to charity. That would keep her mind on reality and take the mystery out of the old armoire!

Just then she heard the telephone ring. Celine, in the lower hall, answered it.

"Miss Heather?" she called. "It's for you."

Heather picked up the extension in her room. Malcolm's voice came cheerfully over the line.

"Hi. I'm suffering from writer's block today. Can't work at all. How about stealing away with me?"

Heather smiled, thankful for his normalcy, his humor. "Malcolm, I don't imagine it takes *too* much of a block to get you to play hooky—"

"Hey! You've got to remember that I'm a serious sort of guy. And I take a beautiful day like this one seriously. Come on, what do you say? I'll contribute the picnic, if you'll grab one of those rather fine bottles of wine you have in the cellar—"

"All right. Anyway, there's something I want to talk to you about."

"Good. Half an hour, then? We'll head up the highway to the mountains. Go for a glorious hike."

"Good idea. I'll unpack my boots."

Heather did just that. Hiking is a popular oc-
cupation in alpine countries, and her parents had
taken her often when she was very young. In
college, she had continued to climb in the Adiron-
dacks and the Green Mountains of Vermont.

Malcolm was a little taken aback when she
appeared at the door, sturdily shod for a strenous
walk through mountain ravines and meadows.
"Oh, no! A professional!" he cried in dismay.

"Only a grimly determined amateur. Where
would you like to go?"

"You know the territory, remember?"

Heather was decisive. "Let's drive up to the Evolène. It's less than twenty miles to the top of the
valley. They decided to take Heather's car. She
would drive up, and he would take the wheel on
the return trip.

Climbing in hairpin turns, they were soon
looking down at Sion and its fortified heights of
Valère and Tourbillion. A light mist still shrouded
the towers, and crept up the twin peaks. They
drove in happy silence, Heather concentrating on
the road.

They passed through the tunnel of the Pyramids
of Euseigne, and Heather explained that the strange
rock pillars had been cut out by erosion. The road
narrowed as they entered the Hérens valley, ringed
by five high mountains.

Women were working the fields in little groups.
They wore traditional costumes, discarded these
days almost everywhere else in Switzerland. In
spite of their colorful dresses, edged with ribbons
and embroidery, the women of the Evolène led a
harsh life on their mountain farms. Heather tried to
imagine how some of her idealistic classmates at

Boston University would react to the extremes of temperature and the demanding physical toil, day after day. . . .

Malcolm was delighted. "They're like rustic Amazons!" he shouted as he happily watched them herding dark brown cows. Some rode on mule back, and some pitched hay into neat piles. "Where are all the men?"

"They work in the lumber mills, mostly," Heather said, laughing.

Malcolm was pointing to the fine old chalets, brown as the alpine cows, and as venerable as the little community itself. They were painstakingly adorned with bright painted flowers, in a gesture of defiance against wind and weather.

The picturesque disorder of Les Haudères came into view. The chalets were set this way and that, without concession to modern ideas of town planning. Malcolm was pleased, and wanted to stop, but Heather drove on. "We've still got a few miles to go," she teased.

He was like an overgrown boy with his bony knees jammed under the dashboard of her compact little car. The wind whipped his sandy hair wildly around, making him the very picture of youthful enthusiasm. *Yet he must be well into his twenties*, she thought, startled at how little she really knew about him.

"We're going up to Ferpècle, where the real mountaineers go," Heather announced. "We can take a stroll in the forest—just to get you into condition."

Malcolm rolled his eyes in mock dismay. "You'd be surprised what condition I'm in! Why, I'm one of the better hikers and skiers where I come from. . . ."

"And where is that?" Heather asked loudly and pointedly over the steady throb of the engine.

"Why, Inverness, of course. The highest of the highlands. You don't think I'm a stranger to this kind of country, do you?" Malcolm leaned back and craned his neck. Above them glowered Dent Blanche, a superb rock pyramid that offered many challenges to adventurous climbers. They had passed the village, and Heather began to look for a place to park. They drove onto a rough gravel clearing off the road, and pulled up under the trees. Malcolm clambered out, stretching elaborately.

"This is the real thing," he exclaimed. "Just smell that air!"

Heather was already drinking it in, deeply and thankfully. The forest whispered around them, tossing resin into the sun-drenched bowl of the valley below. "Come on, then, let's march!"

They each shouldered a little knapsack filled with picnic delicacies. Malcolm slung his camera around his neck; then he was ready.

They set off briskly, following a well-marked trail. Deep among the trees they lost sight of the brooding face of the mountain. Heather knew that the stone giant, like all mountains in this staggering, soaringly beautiful country, had its moods, its own weathers and idiosyncrasies. It was treacherous sometimes, but always magnificent. She clambered exuberantly up the steep trail.

"Take it easy, will you? I haven't got mountain boots on, like you," Malcolm moaned. But he was close behind her, and seemed to be taking the trail easily enough.

They had climbed steadily for more than an hour—up a trail soft with decaying needles and fringed with ferns and hesitant wildflowers—when they came to a broad, open meadow. It stretched before them in the sun, a light wind sweeping the grass. Butterflies flickered here and there over the sudden profusion of flowers.

"Gosh," said Malcolm, "you almost expect yodelers and milkmaids."

"More likely tourists," Heather laughed. "Look . . . there's the road again."

"Why didn't you *tell* me we could drive up? Just for that, you can open the wine. We're having lunch." With that, he plunked down on the grass and began to dig into his knapsack.

Heather was surveying the meadow with its ring of rocky walls. "I've been here before, I know it. Lots of time . . . ."

"But?"

"But I don't remember that chalet over there. Of course, I must have been here the last time my parents sent me for the summer, when I was twelve. . . ."

"And you are now the very great age of about twenty—"

"Twenty-two."

"So that means that whoever had the temerity to build that chalet has had ten years to do so. No wonder you don't remember it." Malcolm munched heartily on his cheese and crusty bread. "Say, am I going to get my wine or not?"

"*You* open it, lazy. I wish I could get a better look at that place. It looks very new, actually. And strange, for a chalet. Well, not strange, but it's not really a chalet, not all woody and 'Swiss.' Do you see all the glass? It must be ninety percent windows."

"Tell you what," said Malcolm. "We'll wander

over there after we've eaten. Sit down and share this wine and loaf with me. Now where did I put that jug?"

"You mean Omar Khayyám's jug?"

" 'A jug of wine, a loaf of bread—and thou . . .' " began Malcolm.

"I thought college Lotharios stopped quoting that one a thousand years ago," Heather said kindly. She sat cross-legged and nibbled the excellent cheese and fruit Malcolm had brought.

"Well, I'm new at it," replied Malcolm. "And I never went to college."

"How do you get to be a writer without going to college?"

"For the stuff I write, the school of hard knocks is best."

"Maybe the thrillers, but what about the historical research you're doing? You told me it was a scholarly effort."

"It is," said Malcolm quickly. "It'll put me on the intellectual map at last."

"You're putting me on, Malcolm. I don't know whether to believe you or not. I'll bet you had some sinister reason for spying on my house yesterday and you made up that story about 'research' on the spot."

"Aha! I knew you'd find me out. You're a clever girl, but you'll see. When my weighty book comes out I'll autograph you a copy. Provided you pay for it."

Heather sighed loudly. "Listen. There's something important that I want to tell you about. But you have to listen, and not kid about it, because . . . because I'm a bit frightened . . . ."

Malcolm looked at her, and his blue eyes were solemn. "Okay, tell me. What is it?"

"It's the house. Or something about the house. Something I don't understand." She told him about the noises she had heard in the night. How the first time she had thought she'd been dreaming. And how, last night, she had been too frightened to make more than a cursory search for their cause. "But I can't imagine what they could be," she finished in a small voice. She felt rather foolish discussing such things aloud, here in the shining mountain meadow.

Malcolm spoke softly, abstractedly. "So . . . a haunted house. 'There are more things in heaven and earth.' Rattling chains and hideous groans . . . ."

"No. Just muted sounds, vague things. Please, Malcolm."

He looked at her steadily for a moment. "Sorry. So Celine wasn't anywhere to be found, you say?"

"She claimed she was sound asleep."

"Hmm. And yet she watches you like a hawk, other times. Strange, but she's strange from the word go, right?"

"Well, she's all common sense about this. Says it's rats."

"Now there's someone with no imagination at all," said Malcolm with a grimace.

"The thing is, she's right. She must be right."

Malcolm paused to take a thoughtful sip of wine. "Look. I don't know what to say. You were frightened; that's all that matters right now. We'll do something about it. I promise we'll get to the bottom of it." He paused again, staring into space. "Your bedroom is on the wall shared by the 'old' house. And the wardrobe is on the wall. . . ." He stood up decisively. "Well, I'll tell you what one of my fictional detectives would do. He'd go into that house and have a look at things. That's what I asked you to let me do yesterday, and now you're going to have to let me do it."

"*We'll* do it, Malcolm. I know that old place, how it's deserted and crumbling and nothing but a wreck. I want to prove it to you. We'll have to yank off a couple of boards to get in."

"What if Celine disapproves?"

"I'll tell her we're just checking the rat situation." Heather helped Malcolm pack up the remains of their picnic. "Anyway, I don't trust her. If she acts funny about it, I'll know she's up to something."

"Why don't you just fire her?"

"Malcolm, you can't deprive a woman of her livelihood just because she's got a sour face. I won't let her intimdate me, that's all."

"Okay, so we play detectve. Maybe we'll find out why she's always fixing you with the evil eye," Malcolm said, shouldering his knapsack.

Heather laughed. "They still talk a lot about witches around here! Sometimes it's positively medieval. Probably the result of all the religious wars a couple of centuries back: Calvinist versus Catholic."

"You're not used to that sort of thing in America, I guess."

"Well, perhaps not, but they did burn a few witches in a town not far from where I live—in Salem."

"Makes you shiver just to think about it. But things were settled long ago, about the time Sion became a market town instead of a seat of power for the bishops. Nobody takes that sort of conflict seriously anymore."

"You *hope*," Heather said. They began to wander across the meadow, toward the strange building Heather wanted to inspect. Heather shook off the dark tentacles of past superstitions. She knew that some people in Sion still clung to them, but that could have little to do with her on this perfect, sunny day in the Alps.

"I'm sure," she announced, "that Celine's diagnosis is correct. All we have to do is prove it to me so I can sleep nights."

Malcolm eyed her. "Good girl. Now let's clear up this current mystery." They were near the building now, and Heather could see that it had been recently built to unconventional standards. Windows glinted everywhere, tilting toward the sky, soaking up the sun. The view from inside must be breathtaking.

There were wooden surfaces, too, complementing the glass, and potted flowers bobbed their heads in the alpine breeze. A garden had been laid out, possibly for vegetables or flowers. The building was obviously expensive, but it was not luxurious. Everything about it had a sense of functionalism, even of self-sufficiency.

"Looks like it belongs to some rich health nut," said Malcolm dryly. "I wonder if they mind us peering in this way."

"We're not peering in. You can't see a thing in this sun. Besides, when did you develop scruples?"

Malcolm looked a little embarrassed. But he unslung his camera and aimed it at the building. "The old and the new," he announced. "Nice contrast for my book." The camera clicked several times.

It was Heather's turn to be embarrassed. "Good heavens, what if they see us? It's this sort of thing that gives tourists a bad name."

"We're not tourists."

"That makes it even worse. They'll *think* we

are—Malcolm, look out! There's a car coming!"
Heather yanked at his arm. They began to walk
away from the road, making every effort to look
nonchalant.

The vehicle turned out to be a small bus, similar
to the vans people like to trek all over in on their
vacations. As it passed, Heather could see that it
was loaded with children. And she saw something
else that made her stand still in her tracks.

Dr. Valdemar was driving the bus! He looked
carefree and relaxed as the breeze whipped the dark
hair from his forehead. One arm was slung across
the back of the seat as he drove, and a little dark-
haired child stood behind him.

His white, flashing smile fixed itself instantly in
her mind. It was an unbelievable contrast to the
scowl she'd first seen on his face. And he hardly
seemed the same man who'd treated her so coolly,
so dismissively in Oscar's shop. Heather almost
wouldn't have known him, if he hadn't made such
a deep impression both times that they'd met.

Somehow she sensed that the man with the smile
was the real Dr. Valdemar, not the aloof and
cyncial person he chose to portray. She stood,
transfixed, and watched as the minibus unloaded
its population of children. They were a quiet little
group, she thought, all walking toward the front
door of the modern building. They scrambled and
clambered and dropped things and trailed behind.
Heather could see that they were all sizes and
several ages. They made an oddly beautiful picture,
clustered around the tall, broad-shouldered man.

A woman in a white uniform greeted the group.
Faintly, Heather could hear her voice, then the
doctor's.

Malcolm's voice, very near, startled her. "So

that's it. It's the new clinic," he said. "Heard about it in town. That must be Anton Valdemar."

"New clinic?" Heather asked, still watching as the last of the children went inside and the door closed.

"Yes, so I hear. The fellow's well-off, they say. Built this place for kids with severe health problems. I gather the man's something of an enigma. Should be practicing in the big city, raking in pots of dough," Malcolm said, taking her arm. "But he stays here, working with these kids. Does that satisfy your curiosity?"

Heather nodded, smiling distractedly at Malcolm. As they walked across the meadow to the forest trail, her mind was drawn powerfully back to images of the clinic, the quiet children, and most of all, to the smiling Dr. Anton Valdemar.

Chapter 5

The next morning Heather got up very early. At first she couldn't decide what it was that was making her feel so good, so positive. Then she remembered. There had been no noises last night.

Perhaps every night would be as peaceful as last night. She had gone to bed pleasantly tired from hiking, and had slept soundly. *Just resting up does you a lot of good*, she thought practically, remembering her mother's little lectures on the subject. Even Celine's silent efficiency in the kitchen couldn't put a damper on her mood.

Heather was polite to the woman; but no longer concerned about her sullenness. When she jotted off a note to her mother a little later, Heather didn't mention Celine's strange attitude, nor the puzzling sounds. They *could* be nothing at all—innocuous noises exaggerated out of proportion by the unsettling experience of coming here, by her brooding over recent death. . . .

She told her mother that it had been the right thing to do, to come here now. She admitted that thoughts of Frederic still overwhelmed her with sadness, but added that she was sure the healing process had started already. She had even made a new friend: a young man, funny but sensible. She paused then, imagining her mother's reaction. Would she think that Malcolm represented a possible replacement for Frederic? Well, it would cheer her up, at any rate. Let her think whatever she wished.

She finished the short letter by saying that she was clearing up some of Aunt Rachel's things today. The duty would be saddening, but somehow seeing those old dresses—clothes Aunt Rachel had worn when Heather was a child—helped her to deal with the enigma of death. And the associations were good ones. "There are a few little things I'll put together for you, mother, jewelry and so on, and I'll ship them soon. Please don't worry."

With a flourish, Heather signed the letter and sealed it. She went on to the next task with a sense of accomplishment. Opening the wardrobe, she took firm hold of the old trunk and dragged it toward her.

The dresses, preserved because of their durability and classic styling, had all been carefully folded. The few on top, which she had disturbed two nights ago, Heather shook carefully and laid over a chair. Bits of dried lavender and peppercorns, believed in the old-fashioned manner to protect the clothing from moths, tumbled out. Working slowly, Heather shook each successive garment. They were treasures, in a way, these flowered silks with their padded shoulders; the fine jerseys and worsteds; and the crimped, conservative rayons. Nostalgia overtook Heather as she remembered Aunt Rachel wearing them in various situations

long ago. Sundays at church would produce
flowered splendor, perhaps cabbage roses on black;
at dinner, presiding over the long oak table that
now stood silent in the unused dining room, Rachel
might wear a woolen dress, or, in a rougish mood,
Rachel would even put on this burgundy evening
dress, soft with the sheen of satin . . . Heather
sighed. She would have to stop daydreaming, and
get on with her task.

Burrowing deeper in the old trunk, she came
across shoes, and hats and gloves, all hopelessly
outdated. What would she do with these? Surely
the nuns at the convent in town would have no use
for them—Heather sat back on her heels. Her brisk
and orderly state of mind was fast fading. It
seemed as if she was intruding, somehow, on the
very fabric of her great-aunt's life. . . .

Suddenly a piece of paper lying on the floor
beside her caught her attention. It must have fallen
from the folds of one of the dresses. Slowly, she
reached down and picked it up. It looked like a
letter—yes, part of one, at any rate—written in
Aunt Rachel's unmistakable script. Heather's hands
began to tremble as she took in the first words.

> Maybe I'm losing my mind. I don't know. Until
> now I've never heard voices or anything like
> that. They say old people do. But now they
> come in the night. Strange sounds that seem to
> come from nowhere.

Heather's heart was racing. The sounds! She had not
imagined them at all! Here was Aunt Rachel's word,
confirming the uncanny presence of those sounds.
Heather hardly dared to read on. But her eyes were
drawn inexorably to the next lines.

But these days I'm hearing odd noises all the time, and they seem to be coming from right inside my room. It always happens at night. I turn on my lamp and look around, but there's never anything there. It's always the same. Everything is quiet. Then I start to hear muted, muffled sounds, like—I don't know, like whispers—they come and go, sometimes louder than others. Celine told me it was probably rats next door in the old house, but I don't believe her. I don't know whether to trust her or not. She does her work properly—I can't find fault with that at all. But I wonder—and God help me, isn't this the sort of thing old women always say— sometimes I wonder if she isn't spying on me all the time. I sense something wrong. She doesn't speak, just does her work. I see her looking at me with those strange eyes. And I don't seem to see anyone else anymore. I have the distinct impression that she sends people away. I feel like a prisoner in my house. I hope this letter reaches you, Heather. I am going to go out and mail it myself, because I'm afraid Celine won't send it if I give it to her. . . .

Here, the letter broke off.

Heather stared bleakly at the pitiful words. They seemed to explain Aunt Rachel's "reclusiveness" very well. Celine had treated her just as she was treating Heather now! And the noises: Aunt Rachel had been frightened out of her wits by them.

Out of her wits? Heather hastily corrected herself. The letter sounded perfectly sane; she couldn't believe that Aunt Rachel had become a senile old woman.

Anger seared through Heather. Something would have to be done right away. The letter, though too late to help Rachel, had finally reached its destination. Aunt Rachel had obviously meant to mail it. . . .

In the lower hall, the doorbell rang. Malcolm! Thank goodness!

Now she could show him further evidence of those night sounds. She hurried downstairs, just as Celine was opening the door.

Malcolm was as cheerful as ever, breezily greeting Celine and ignoring her frigid response.

He grinned broadly at Heather. "Come on then, love, today's the day we—"

Quickly Heather broke in. "Come upstairs, Malcolm. There's something I want to show you." She gave him a hard look that meant he was not to say anything in front of Celine.

He looked quizzical for the briefest of moments, then seemed to understand. "Right, then, lead on."

Without acknowledging Celine's cold stare of disapproval, Heather whirled and hurried up the staircase, Malcolm galloping behind her.

"What's up?" he whispered as soon as they were in her room and Heather had closed the door. "Aren't you getting a little paranoid about the woman?"

"You can speak normally, Malcolm. And no, I am not getting paranoid. Look at this." She thrust the letter at him.

Malcolm scanned the page quickly, gave a low whistle, then read it again more slowly. "Wow," he said at length.

He looked steadily at Heather, then frowned. "This seems to tell a pretty sad story, all right. But— now wait—I know what you're thinking, how it must make you feel—"

"How could you?" Heather cried. "You didn't know her—you're a stranger!"

"Okay, okay. But sit down. Try to calm down, Heather."

Heather sat down, but she was trembling with anger.

"Now listen to me," Malcolm urged. "*If* there's anything to this, we'll find out. Believe that. But please consider: there may *not* be anything to it. No, let me finish. Old people tend to exaggerate things sometimes. They often develop persecution complexes. They imagine people are spying on them, plotting against them. And they usually suspect the closest members of their families, or their nurse, companions—those who live with them. Now remember, Celine was the only person your great-aunt saw, day in and day out. It's not surprising she would become the chief suspect if the old lady's imagination started to run away with her."

Heather wouldn't listen to any more.

"You're saying she was crazy!"

"I'm not. But I don't want *you* running off in all directions over this. We've got to take it slowly and find out what really happened. Isn't that what you want?"

"Yes," she said, mollified.

"Please, Heather, trust me. We can't assume that something gothic and sinister has been going on around here until we get hold of something more concrete than this letter."

"Look," said Heather, her voice tired and flat. "I suppose you could be right—except for the fact that *I* heard the noises, and *I* have seen this woman, this Celine Dumas, behave in exactly the manner described. But I will grant that you may be right. I just want to know, that's all. Because when I do know, I'm going to make it up, for Aunt Rachel. Do you understand?"

Malcolm nodded solemnly. "I understand," he

said gently. "Now I think we should go ahead with our plan. We're going to take a look inside the old part of this house right now. If Celine is hiding anything that should make her tip her hand. After all, she didn't encourage you to go there."

Heather looked doubtfully at him. "Shouldn't we do it without her knowing? I mean, if there's anything sinister about her, we want to catch her off guard, surely."

"I don't see that it matters too much. Send her out on an errand if you like. And don't let on that you're angry."

Heather agreed. She made up a list of things for Celine to do in town, and went downstairs to present it to her. Celine looked at Heather with an extra hint of malice, which temporarily puzzled her—until she realized that the woman must be assuming that she was being sent out of the house so that Malcolm and Heather might have privacy. Heather would almost have laughed at the insinuation that she was romantically involved with Malcolm if she hadn't been so angry. Celine had certainly made her Aunt Rachel's life more difficult by ensuring her isolation. Whatever else Celine had done, Heather swore to discover.

Malcolm joined her downstairs, and they waited until Celine had left.

"Now then. We need a hammer or a crowbar," said Malcolm. "What've you got?"

"Let's check the basement," Heather replied.

They found a large, utilitarian flashlight, made sure it worked, and began looking for tools. Malcolm was enjoying poking around in the cellar with her.

"These foundations are ancient," he remarked. "I'll really have to comb the archives—I'll try to

find some old town maps." Heather groped.
"Here's a hammer. Will that do?"

"Let's try it and see." They hurried upstairs and
went outside, around to the courtyard. To reach
the boarded-up outer door of the old house, they
had to pass through the courtyard. Walled and
with a stubbornly rusted gate latch, the yard was
heavily overgrown with weeds. They made their
way to the door, and Malcolm began prying at the
weathered boards nailed across it. The wood
cracked loudly, and nails squealed as they were
torn from rusted anchorages.

"Somebody did a good job on this," he gasped.
"One could hardly slip in here secretly in the dark
of night. Phew!" He paused to mop his brow.

Impatiently Heather took the hammer from him
and began hacking away herself.

"Hey, hey! Take it easy!"

Heather didn't answer. She kept pulling with all
her might at the protesting boards. They refused to
budge. Frustrated, she slumped against the doorway
and stared moodily at Malcolm.

He grinned. "Well, I guess it's better that you
take your anger out on that wood. . . ."

She managed a rueful smile. "Okay, hero, here's
the hammer."

With one mighty effort Malcolm managed to
pull away two boards.

"There's the door to deal with," he said, a little
grimly. "I don't suppose there's a key. . . ."

"Uncle Maurice closed this up years ago . . . I
don't suppose they ever kept one. But maybe.
Hang on." She ran from the courtyard while Malcolm pried away more of the old boards.

Breathlessly Heather ran into the front hall and
began to fumble in the drawer of the table where

she remembered that all manner of things, keys among them, had once been kept. But aside from miscellaneous gloves and pencils there was nothing. Where on earth would it be—if it still existed at all? Heather's heart sank. It was the proverbial needle in the haystack.

Then she had an idea. Old doors like that often had simple keys, iron ones, that fit more than one lock in a house. She would get Celine's key ring, which she usually kept in the kitchen in a certain cupboard. If only she hasn't taken it with her, Heather prayed as she entered the kitchen.

She found the key ring, a very large one, festooned with old keys that couldn't possibly have any current use. Why would Celine keep all these, she wondered.

She hurried back to Malcolm, waving the keys in triumph.

But he was not in sight. Bewildered, Heather looked around the courtyard. Then she noticed that behind the torn splinters of wood there was a gaping blackness. Somehow, he had opened the door.

"Malcolm?"

He poked his head out and grinned disarmingly. "Did it, see? The lock was very rusty."

"I've got keys." She dangled them in front of him.

He took a quick look at them. "Not the sort of thing at all. They probably belong to your inside doors. Bedrooms and things like that. Well, come in." He held out a hand to help her over the lower boards that still barred the doorway.

Heather stepped into the gloom of the old house. It took long moments, even with the flashlight, for her eyes to adjust to the darkness. Damp currents of air seemed to rush by her. There was a heavy, musty smell. Gradually, she began to make out the dimensions of the room. Light crept in through tiny cracks in the boarded windows: thin, sinister beams that could not dispel the oppressive closeness.

"Here it is. The haunted house," announced Malcolm.

Heather's eyes followed the beam of her companion's flashlight as he directed it around the room. Broken-down furniture was stacked in corners. Dusty armchairs slumped, sodden and gray, their upholstery in shreds. Bureaus with drawers slung crookedly out supported stacks of picture frames, twisted clothes hangers, tattered lampshades.

"Untidy, isn't it?" Malcolm asked, swinging the long beam of the flashlight from floor to ceiling. Wallpaper hung in strips here and there, and plaster had tumbled down in piles. Around the ceiling, as Malcolm swung the light, Heather could make out the baroque fantasies of some long-dead plasterer. Shadows floated from those cornices. *Live shadows*, she thought suddenly, involuntarily starting.

"Bats," said Malcolm. "We've woken them up. I hope you're not a sissy."

Heather gulped. "Of course not. I told you, I used to play here as a kid," she said, ducking.

"I wouldn't be surprised if there are rats in here, as well," Malcolm remarked thoughtfully.

"Just let's get on with it, shall we?" Heather tried to cover the nervousness in her voice.

"Okay. I want to check the far wall, all the way up. And the cellar."

"I told you. There is no cellar," said Heather. "There's this room and three other large ones on this floor, I think. Then you go upstairs, and you find more rooms, about as many."

"The ones to pay attention to are the ones along

that wall—the ones next to your house," Malcolm said, walking cautiously forward. "Now look out, these floorboards may not be all they used to . . . ."

Abruptly, Malcolm was pitched forward as one of the very boards he was talking about gave way. There was the sound of splintering wood and a sharp curse as he stumbled. The flashlight flew wierdly through the air and skittered across the room.

Startled, Heather pressed her fist to her mouth. Malcom muttered in the darkness and extricated himself. "That hurt," he growled, reaching for the flashlight. Heather could see only its beam, in the pitch-black.

"We must be near the staircase," she said. "At least the windows give some light.

A hollowed-out face loomed at her. Heather started violently, but almost immediately realized that Malcolm was holding the flashlight up under his chin. She recovered quickly. "It suits you," she said dryly.

"Okay. Let's get down to business," Malcolm said. "You stay here. The staircase is likely to be in the worst condition of all."

"Not on your life. Do you think I want to idle around at the mercy of those bats?"

"I doubt it," sighed Malcolm. "Come on, then. Only be careful."

With extreme caution, they crept up the old staircase. Malcolm flashed the beam carefully, closely inspecting each step. Finally they reached the top without mishap. Heather, however, was unpleasantly aware of the thick coating of dust that lay over everything. She was certain she had walked through dozens of spiderwebs.

The upper rooms were as dim as those downstairs, but they were practically empty except for a few pieces of discarded furniture. Malcolm carefully explored the walls of the rooms that were on the attached side.

"Do you know," he said at last, "there's no sign of anything. Though I don't know what we expected to find." Malcolm shone his light around the floors of the main rooms, and into every corner.

"Solid," he said at last. "Just dust, and no footprints of brigands and murderers. Nobody here but us mice. What do you think of that, Sherlock?"

Heather had had her fill of the stifling darkness. "I think we'd better get out into the fresh air," she said.

They made their way out, feeling disappointed that they hadn't come any closer to solving the noises than earlier.

"Well, that got us exactly nowhere," Heather grumbled, blinking in the sun and brushing herself off.

"Cheer up. Now we know what the noises *aren't*. Nobody's invading the old house at night to scare you out of your wits. Probably it *is* the rats."

"Probably," Heather said, discouraged. "I need a bath."

UP TO HER CHIN in steaming bathwater, Heather brooded unhappily about her great-aunt's unfinished letter. It had been a cry for help, one that Heather must answer, even if it was too late for Aunt Rachel. If the night noises were real, if they meant anything, she must find out what. And if Celine had any sinister purpose for being in the house—if she had really been spying on Aunt Rachel—then Heather must somehow discover why.

What should her next step be? The escapade in the old house had got them nowhere—although, as Malcolm had said, they could at least eliminate the idea of nocturnal intruders other than small animals.

And there were no signs that any human had been in there who had planned to frighten Aunt Rachel—or herself. Not even a footprint; the dust indicated that the house hadn't been disturbed in years.

Heather considered the possibility that someone was making ghostly noises in some other way— perhaps with wires, hooked up to a tape recorder. But why would anyone want to do such a thing? Had somebody wanted Aunt Rachel to leave the house? Maybe there was something they wanted, some treasure, Heather thought hopefully.

Or maybe Celine had planned to manipulate Aunt Rachel—so that she herself might inherit the house. But if that were true she had certainly not succeeded. And yet . . . Celine might be trying to frighten Heather, to ultimately cut her off from the outside world, and then to manipulate her. But how did she think she could do that?

Heather splashed around noisily for a few moments, scrubbing herself and thinking angrily of Celine. *I'll fire her. I'll just tell her to get out, right away. That'll solve it.*

But firing Celine would solve nothing, Heather told herself. If Aunt Rachel's letter had any truth behind it, Heather wanted Celine within easy reach. She must not be allowed to get away with her treatment of a defenseless, sick old woman.

But *no one in our family ever asked about the details of Aunt Rachel's illness,* thought Heather with painful clarity. They had known she suffered from attacks of angina, and that death had been attributed simply to a heart attack. That was all. It hadn't seemed necessary to delve any deeper.

But what if there was something else? Shouldn't she make it her business to check into the circumstances of Aunt Rachel's death a little more thoroughly?

It was a good idea, Heather realized. In fact, this was the next logical step. She would find out what the doctor, the good Dr. Valdemar himself, thought of Aunt Rachel's mental state.

She stood up in the huge old claw-footed bathtub and began to dry herself. The water gurgled loudly down the drain, echoing in the steamy room. She stepped carefully onto the mat.

But I know what Dr. Valdemar thinks about that. He thinks she was getting dotty, too. He said so, the other day in Oscar's shop! Heather's heart sank. Maybe it was true, after all.

She remembered Malcolm's cautioning words about old people and their persecution complexes. His interpretation was reasonable; she was forced to admit that. But she couldn't deny the nudgings of her own first instincts—her perception of a sense of wrongness in this house. And she couldn't deny the pathetic letter Aunt Rachel had never mailed.

She would go to see the doctor.

Once her mind was made up, Heather admitted to herself that she was very nervous indeed. Some quality or air about the man had put her off balance, right from the start. His powerful, tense physique seemed to contain a deep anger, barely controlled, to which she had already been exposed.

But then she remembered the last time she had seen him. Smiling, surrounded by children. A happy man . . . a contradictory man.

While she dressed, carefully selecting and discarding several outfits. Heather focused on that smiling face. It made it easier, somehow, to plan what she was going to say. Several elaborate possibilities ran through her mind, but finally she decided the best thing would be the simple truth. She was disturbed about her aunt's mental state at the time of her death—could he throw any light on it?

She drove the twenty miles or so to the clinic in the mountain pasture, trying all the while to quell the unsettled feeling that came over her when she thought about Anton Valdemar. She attempted to analyze it. After all, he was an extremely attractive man, in spite of his aloofness.

But she still loved Frederic; perhaps would always love Frederic. So there was no reason for this butterfly feeling in her stomach—nothing, except Dr. Valdemar's hard-bitten exterior. Therefore there was no reason why she shouldn't be able to deal civilly with him as one mature human being to another.

Heather resolved to be absolutely businesslike. On this confident note, she approached the clinic along the road that cut through the high pasture. There were a few vehicles parked out front, so she pulled up alongside the nearest. As she walked along the path that circled the parking space, she could see a few children off in the meadow, playing. The woman in the white uniform was with them. Coming to broad wooden steps, Heather paused to take a deep breath.

Before she had started up, however, one of the cedar and glass doors swung violently open. A blond woman, exquisitely tailored in the latest "country" fashion from Paris, strode out, her face a study in seething rage. For a couple of breathless seconds, Heather was stunned.

The woman was Geraldine! Geraldine herself, the sleek, lacquered Geraldine of those glamorous parties—Geraldine who, Heather had been sure, had slyly tried to take Frederic from her.

What on earth would Geraldine be doing *here*?

Heather was rooted to the spot, too startled to make a move one way or the other. Geraldine was pelting down the steps with furious haste; the collision was inevitable.

"Look out, can't you?" Geraldine snapped as she turned angrily to get a better look at this person who had had the stupidity to get in her way. Then the anger fell from her face like a mask, to be replaced with a thin, calculating malice.

"Good Lord," she said. "It's the little American— the girl from Boston U., Heather, isn't it?"

"That's right," Heather said stiffly.

"Frederic's friend. Poor Frederic. But what are you doing way up here in Heidi country? The people one meets! I just can't believe it!"

"Well, I'm here to see Dr. Valdemar, actually," Heather said, blushing furiously at her own meekness. She shouldn't even be polite to this woman! How could Geraldine talk about Frederic so offhandedly?

"I didn't know you had a neurotic kid," Geraldine said with a superior little smile.

In spite of herself, Heather looked puzzled. "A neurotic kid? I—I don't have a child at all."

Geraldine's smirk widened knowingly. "Really . . . why else would you be here? That's the only thing my husband does these days—he looks after nutty kids."

"Your husband?" Heather heard herself ask stupidly, already knowing the answer.

"Anton. Dr. Valdemar to you. And don't look

so shocked, just because you never saw me with a husband in Paris. I grew out of this mountain backwater years ago. . . . But I must run, no time to stand around and chat. Good luck with the bear in there." Geraldine was obviously in a great rush. She strode over to a large, expensive and very powerful sedan and drove off with an inelegant roar. Heather stared after her, dumbfounded. Geraldine—of all people in the whole world—here? And Dr. Valdemar was her husband!

Heather recalled that Geraldine had been introduced to her by some other surname in Paris, but she couldn't remember what it was.

The car had disappeared around a far bend, into the forest, but Heather stared numbly after it, trying to absorb this new development.

The clinic door swung open, and Heather turned to see Anton Valdemar looking blankly at her for a moment. Then he stared down the road and scowled deeply.

This was obviously not the best day to have come! But Heather summoned all her courage. It was no concern of hers what his personal problems might be; she had a professional matter to discuss with him.

"Dr. Valdemar," she began. "There's something I'd like to see you about. . . ."

He stared down at her in a distracted way, then seemed to see her for the first time. "Miss Ashley, isn't it?" he asked. His voice was low and brusque.

"Yes. I wanted to—"

"Don't let's discuss it here," he said shortly. "Come inside." He held the door wide for her to enter. Heather hurried past him into the clinic.

Inside, one had the feeling of being completely open to the outdoors. Sunlight poured in everywhere, and the views from all angles were as heartstopping as she had imagined they would be. "How beautiful," breathed Heather, without thinking.

Anton Valdemar was watching her. "Yes," he said. "Now, what did you want to talk to me about?"

Heather felt her cheeks burning. His eyes were compelling, and held a bleak, strained look. What she had to say had better be important! "I've come about my aunt—my great-aunt, Rachel Savorin."

The doctor's eyes flickered very slightly, Heather thought, but he said nothing.

"I'm concerned about her—about her state of mind in the last months of her life."

"Well, come in then, come in and sit down." He led her to an inner office that faced the mountain side of the little pasture. The office was furnished with austere simplicity, but papers lay everywhere, piled in a sort of orderly confusion. Dr. Valdemar was forced to clear off a chair so that Heather might sit. "I seldom hold consultations anymore," he explained.

Heather sat. The only personal touch she could detect in the office was a small framed photograph of a dark-haired child.

The doctor sat down opposite her and looked directly into her eyes. "Just what is it that's bothering you, Miss Ashley? You say you're worried about your great-aunt's mental state, what she was like around the time of her death? I believe I remarked the other day that she seemed— reclusive, a bit odd, in the manner of elderly people. I can't go much beyond that, I'm afraid."

"Also, I . . . I wanted to know more about the exact cause of her death," Heather blurted. Would he see her interest as a reflection of his skills as a physician?

He frowned. "Without becoming entirely

technical, I can tell you that Rachel Savorin died of a massive coronary occlusion—a heart attack." He stood up and went to a filing cabinet behind him. One of the drawers yielded a thin brown folder. He laid it flat on the desk.

Sitting down again, he scanned the file. Heather could see that there wasn't a great deal in it. "Dr. Mazarell has most of her records—any that go back for most of her medical history. Mine relate only to the period during which I treated her. However, I incorporated relevant data. Let's see— incidence of angina pectoris . . . senile dementia—"

"That means senility, doesn't it?" interrupted Heather.

The doctor nodded.

"Do you think she was senile? That she could have had persecution fantasies?"

"It's possible," Dr. Valdemar said. "At least the second is possible. I did not regard her as senile, however. The reference in my notes was just speculation."

On a sudden impulse Heather dug into her handbag and took out the letter. "I'd like you to read this, please. It's not dated, but I'm sure it was written within a few months of Aunt Rachel's death, by her."

He read silently for a moment or two. At last he looked up, his eyes solemn. "This must be saddening for you, Miss Ashley. But I hope you don't take it seriously. It is consistent with the state of mind of many elderly people when they are confined or when they see no one for months at a time. It is in fact consistent with things your aunt said to me."

"She told you about the noises?"

"I was forced to discount her story—or at least

to attribute the noises not to some sinister source, but to rodents in the walls. In such an old house, it's to be expected. No one but Mrs. Savorin ever heard the noises. . . ."

"What would you say if I told you I've heard them myself?"

He looked at her calmly. "I would say that you, too, have heard rats."

"And I know this woman, Celine Dumas. She's exactly the way my aunt describes her."

"Then I would say that you have an extremely unpleasant housekeeper. Look, I can see that you're completely crestfallen at the idea that there might be some perfectly ordinary explanation for this very sad letter. But you shouldn't be. There is unhappiness in old age, but it would be much compounded if helpless old women fell victim to all the plots they themselves imagine." And he smiled at her in a strange, gentle way, as if he were thinking of something else.

"I expect you're right," Heather said slowly. "In fact, I'll be glad if you're right." She stood up briskly. "I've taken enough of your time. I'll go now."

"It's entirely right that you should have come to me. Don't apologize." The doctor's aloofness had returned. He rose and escorted Heather out of the office. As they stepped into the larger room they had first entered, the children came in from the fields with their nurse.

Dr. Valdemar watched them file through the entrance hall. Heather noticed that his face had softened. She found herself sharing his pleasure at the entrance of the children.

"They're all such little individuals," she remarked without thinking.

"Yes," he replied in an absent tone. "I only wish we could treat them more individually." Suddenly he seemed to realize she was an outsider. He frowned. "I only meant that we're a little understaffed here. I didn't mean to bring up my problems in the midst of your own, Miss Ashley. Can I show you to your car?"

Heather, feeling dismissed, drove down the road from the clinic without paying much attention to what she was doing. She was thinking what a strange combination Geraldine and Dr. Valdemar were.

Her thoughts naturally turned to the quarrel that had obviously taken place between them before her arrival. Their relationship certainly couldn't have been a happy one, if that was any indication. . . . Geraldine, she knew, traveled a great deal. Whenever Heather had seen her in the past, there was nothing in her manner or speech that even hinted the woman was married.

It had come as a great shock to Heather to learn that Geraldine was actually married . . . and to Dr. Valdemar! They seemed such an unlikely couple. For some reason Heather couldn't define she found herself feeling vaguely disappointed in Dr. Valdemar. But he had probably discovered life with a woman like Geraldine could be extremely difficult. Had he ever regretted his marriage, she wondered. And how long had they been married? Swerving dangerously on a curve, she was forced to return her attention to driving.

Chapter 6

That night, when the noises began, Heather was ready for them. She sat up in bed, every nerve taut, hardly daring to breath. She listened for a few moments to be sure . . . yes, there it was again. A muffled thumping sound.

It seemed impossible—they had found nothing disturbing in the deserted old house. But Heather was sure the noises came from the other side of her bedroom wall. And this sound was somehow different from those she had heard before. It had a sharper, more measured quality.

It was now or never. Heather made up her mind to find out once and for all what was going on. If she could only catch whoever—or whatever—was making the sounds *while* the sound were being made. . . .

Stealthily, she slipped out of bed. Without turning on the lamp, she felt for her robe and slippers and carried them with her out of the room. She made her way soundlessly along the hall and down the stairs. Her heart was beating quickly, and she could feel a damp coldness in her palms.

She put on her slippers, which were snug and pliable and would not scuff as she walked, and threw the robe across her shoulders.

She was determined, this time, to find some answers to the puzzle hidden in the house. If the old section proved to be empty . . . well, she would then be forced to start believing in ghosts.

With rigid caution, she turned the knob on the front door. It made a small squeak, and she froze, listening. The house remained silent. She turned the knob the rest of the way and quickly stepped out into the night. She dared not close the door completely; there *would* be a noise then, a sharp click as the nightlock slipped into place. She left the door very slightly open.

Outside she took a deep breath of the night air, now strange and earth-smelling, and full of small whisperings. She must remain calm—must move as silently as the tree shadows that surrounded her.

She rounded the corner of the courtyard and stepped through the open gate. Walking noise-lessly, she approached the door, now only half-boarded. The entrance was in still deeper shadow. Trembling, Heather put her hand through the space in the boards. Would she touch wood . . . was the door closed?

She found no barrier. The door was open! She had checked it only a few hours before when she came home. It had been securely locked then. A chill passed through her body. She had an urge to turn and run away. She wasn't so certain now that she wanted answers badly enough to go blindly inside . . . to face whatever lay waiting in the blackness. Every instinct warned that there was danger here.

Why hadn't she brought the flashlight? But if she

went back for it now, she ran the risk of being heard—and using a light would sacrifice the element of surprise.

She couldn't allow herself to hesitate any longer, or she would lose her nerve entirely. Very carefully Heather stepped over the wooden barricade and into the stifling dark of the old house.

She could see absolutely nothing. There were not even the tiny slivers of light admitted by the boarded-up windows in the daytime. There was nothing but utter blackness.

As a blind person might, Heather reached her hands out. Slowly, cautiously, she walked into the darkness ahead. She tried desperately to remember where the old furniture had been. She felt ahead with her toes before taking each step; straining to hear those oddly familiar noises.

There wasn't a sound, except for the trip-hammer beating of her own heart. There was nothing to guide her toward her quarry except her own senses. . . .

She stopped. Her heart seemd to skip a beat. A horrible, tingling sensation ran through her, and with it came the realization that she was not alone.

Someone was here, very near in the darkness. She was not the hunter, but the hunted. She dared not breathe. A cry rose within her, threatened to choke her. But somehow she held it back. She stood very still, her eyes wide, alert. But she could see nothing, hear nothing. She had only an intuitive animal certainty that someone *was* there.

Her mind raced. She should step backward, back out into the night; she should run. But in the silence, she realized that whoever was in this room with her was watching, too, as frozen as she. And just as unable to see.

To panic now and run would accomplish nothing. She must steel herself, must not allow herself to be frightened. And she had to find a way to force whoever this unknown person was to reveal himself. Or *herself*, Heather amended with an inner chill.

Time seemed to stretch unbearably in the black silence. There was no sound, no movement. She breathed shallowly—silently, she hoped. Her shoulders ached from standing so rigidly. Soon she must make some overt move, must speak—and reveal her exact position—before any more of those agonizing moments could pass.

But Heather was spared the necessity of doing anything at all about the terror-filled impasse. The other person moved suddenly, and very quickly, lunging past her toward the gray patch that was the opening in the door. Every nerve in Heather's body tensed. She heard the footsteps, loud on the ancient floorboards; felt the small repellent brush of the stranger's body warmth. But still she saw nothing.

Her head jerked around automatically, following the sound of the footsteps. There was a shadow, just the swiftest glimpse, in front of the doorway. Then even the shadow was blotted out as the heavy wooden door swung shut. There was a sharp click as the lock fell into place.

Almost in the same instant Heather found her voice. "What do you think you're doing?" she cried into the silence. She rushed in the direction of the door, shouting. "Who are you? *Answer me!*" But there was no response, except a brief receding scuffle of feet on the flagstones of the courtyard outside. Frantically, Heather felt for the door handle. She struggled angrily with its unyielding, rusty lock. It was no use. She had been locked in!

She worked at the handle, turning it this way and that, pulling and pushing and twisting. But her blind movements brought no result.

Heather gritted her teeth furiously, and hot tears of frustration sprang to her eyes. Locked in! She was trapped, here with the dust and bats, the rats and heaven knew what else. Heather struggled with the childhood fears that washed over her—of spiders and small scurrying things, and of the dark itself.

She shouted a few times, calling Celine. But after several tries, she realized that she could not be heard—or that Celine chose not to hear her.

There was nothing to do but wait for daylight.

Heather shuddered, drawing her robe tightly around her. It would be along night—surely the longest of her life. Hysteria threatened to engulf her as she thought of the things that shared the darkness with her. She realized she must force her mind to be orderly and calm.

Very carefully, she sat down, with her back against the door. She would spend her time, the long, black hours of this night, pondering the problem at hand, she told herself sternly. Who had been here?

Her suspicions were focused on Celine. But it hardly seemed possible that Celine had locked her in. The intruder had moved decisively, and with the agility of physical strength. Celine was well into middle age—she must be nearing sixty, in fact. Although she was strong enough, and still did heavy household work regularly, she was tall, angular and thin. Certainly she seemed incapable of moving as quicky as the unknown person had. But perhaps under stress . . . .

Who else might it have been? A stranger, a
casual trespasser—someone from town who had
noticed the boards removed from the doorway,
and with visions of plunder had decided on a
burglary attempt. . . . Such a person would quite
naturally have run off, and locked the door, as
well, to prevent Heather from identifying them.

The locked door . . . that was strange. How
would a stranger get inside, when the door had
been locked this afternoon? The lock was perfectly
sound, and that, too, was odd. Malcolm had
forced it, broken it, presumably, to get in without
a key. Yet now it worked perfectly. It was obvious
that Malcolm, for some reason, had lied about the
lock. He hadn't forced it, after all.

Why would he lie? *Could it be that Malcolm was
the intruder*? The thought was so sudden and
unexpected that Heather gave a start. Malcolm was
in many ways secretive. He claimed to be a writer,
but as far as Heather could tell he never wrote
anything. And there was his deep interest in the
house that first day. The spying from the tree!

There was something *wrong*, somehow. Malcolm
seemed to talk in one manner and behave in
another. What was he hiding? Certainly if he got
into the old house yesterday without a key, he
could have done it again tonight. And though he
often pretended to be awkward she had seen him
move with the speed and agility of a cat. It could
have been Malcolm who had run past her in the
darkness.

Just wait till I get out of here, Heather said
fiercely to herself. *I'm going to settle a few things
with Mr. Malcolm McBride!*

Heather drew her knees up and hugged herself in
the dark. It wasn't pleasant to think that Malcolm
might be hiding some interest of his own in the

house. She had trusted him; she didn't want to think too deeply about what his behavior might mean.

For the next few hours she sat in the same spot, listening for noises, thinking angry thoughts and—to her own surprise—occasionally dozing off.

At last, very gradually, gray light began to steal in through the narrow spaces in the boarded windows. Heather could begin to make out objects in the room. The blackest shadows receded from the decaying old furniture, and she could see well enough to move around. She must find something to work on the door with. She must get out of here, and quickly.

Exploring carefully, Heather went through the drawers of the old bureaus. This she did with trepidation and distaste, for it was evident that mice had nested there for several years.

She poked around in the piles of boxes. There must be something here that would be useful: a hammer, or a screwdriver, or even a knife. On top of a time-scarred table her hand touched metal. She picked the object up hopefully. It was a screwdriver! A large sturdy one, too. She was entitled to *some* luck, after all!

She hurried to the door and spent the next half hour experimenting with the lock. She tried forcing it this way and that, and finally something gave. She was able to wedge the tool in and turn the stubborn handle.

The lock would have to be replaced later, she decided, but until then she would nail it shut.

With a sigh of deep relief she stepped out into the morning, just as the birds began their caroling.

"YOU LOOK A BIT TIRED, you know," Malcolm said, his expression one of concerned innocence. They were having lunch in town at the courtyard of the old inn. Heather had been picking at her salad, and now she twisted her wineglass by its stem, moodily watching the reflections in its depths.

"Well, thank you very much," she said in an injured tone.

"Hey, I didn't mean it that way. What's the matter? More noises last night?"

She looked up at him. "Yes, as a matter of fact." Was there a guilty flicker deep in that steady blue gaze? "Yes, there were noises. And they were not a product of my imagination."

Malcolm looked puzzled. "I just can't figure it out. It must be rats. . . ."

"It's not rats," Heather said firmly.

His eyebrows lifted. "How do you know?"

She watched him for along moment. Malcolm was sincere. He would never have locked her in that terrifying place. Her suspicions of the night before were evaporating, becoming formless. In a way she was relieved. She could tell him about the intruder; together they could use their common sense to sort out what had happened. "Last night, I heard the sounds again, only this time—" She stopped in the middle of her sentence.

Geraldine had strolled into the inn yard. She was accompanied by a man whose deep tan and gold neck chains had a look more often seen on the French Riviera than here in staid old Sion. Geraldine permitted her escort to seat her. Then her gaze swept the courtyard with cool and narrowed eyes, stopping to rest for a brief moment on Heather. Her lips formed a small, condescending smile, and she nodded, ever so slightly, then turned to speak to the man. Heather had been dismissed.

"You look as though you've seen a ghost," she

heard Malcolm say. He jerked around awkwardly, and very obviously, to see for himself what Heather was looking at.

"Malcolm, for God's sake, don't stare! Let's get out of here." Heather pushed her chair back. "Hurry!"

"All right, all right. But I don't see what—"

"Never mind. Just come on." And without looking back she hurried from the courtyard. Malcolm fumbled with the check, then sprinted a short distance to catch up with her. He took her arm to slow her down.

"Now, suppose you explain that little drama. I'm awfully curious." He was grinning, but Heather couldn't smile back. She knew that her face was burning with color. She didn't trust herself to speak.

"Who was that woman?" he prompted.

"Just someone I used to know," Heather replied without inflection.

"She looked like quite a sophisticated number to me. That nail polish and those dangly earrings. Probably a chic Parisienne. Am I right?"

"You are. She's from Paris, and I knew her because my fiancé, Frederic, used to go to a lot of parties, and she was always there. . . ."

Malcolm stood still, seemingly oblivious of the busy shoppers flowing past them in the street. "Your fiancé? You never said you were engaged."

"I'm not, not any more. Frederic died . . . he was killed in a car accident."

Malcolm's gaze clouded. "I'm terribly sorry."

"I've been trying not to think about it, you see, and now she comes along again. . . ."

"What has she got to do with it?"

Heather began to walk again. The old tightening

had risen in her throat. "Nothing, really. She has nothing to do with it. Except . . . the day Frederic died, I started a terrific argument with him because—because I was jealous. Jealous of *her*. I saw them together. It was all innocent, I know, but I exaggerated everything . . . . I made him angry."

Malcolm put an arm around her shoulders. "You poor kid," he said.

Heather couldn't seem to stop the words now that they had begun. "He . . . he was angry, and he slammed out to his car. He drove off, and he couldn't have been paying any attention at all, because there was a crash. Oh, I just wish I'd never, ever said those things. . . ." She was crying freely now. Malcolm drew her into a doorway and produced a large white handkerchief.

Heather fought to control her weeping, while he placed his lanky frame between her and curious eyes. At last she looked bleakly up at him. "This is terrible. I'm sorry—"

He shushed her immediately. "All you've got to do is to get over the idea that it was your fault, too. It wasn't, you know. Guys who take their feelings out behind the wheel of a car should expect disaster. . . ."

"Don't talk about Frederic that way!"

Malcolm looked grim for a moment. "Sorry," he said.

Heather dabbed a last time at her eyes. "Let's go," she said.

Malcolm walked along beside her, his hands jammed into his pockets, and his shoulders hunched.

Heather's thoughts tumbled amiss. Nothing seemed to make any sense. "And do you know what?" she said at last, as if to herself.

"What?"

"She's married. Married to that man we saw the other day. Dr. Valdemar."

Malcolm stopped and stared at her, again in surprise. "She *is*? How on earth do you know that?"

"I saw her. I spoke to her, and she told me so. . . . Yesterday, at his clinic. I went up to Ferpècle. I wanted to see him—about the letter. Aunt Rachel's letter."

"He was her doctor?"

"Yes. For a while, at any rate. He treated her at the time of her death."

"Curiouser and curiouser," mused Malcolm. "And what did he say?"

"He said what you said. That old women get persecution complexes."

"Well, they do, you know."

"Not in this case. I'm convinced of that. I know there was something wrong going on at that house. Aunt Rachel was really terrified." Heather stopped and looked at him squarely. "I'm going to find out what it was, and who is responsible."

Malcolm gave a funny little nod and started walking again. "Yes, well, I've been looking into the background of that house. I suspect the old part was built in the fifteenth century, around the same time as the cathedral."

"That's all very romantic, Malcolm, but it just fuzzes up the real problem. I want to know what's going on there in the present." Heather shuddered inwardly, as images of last night filled her mind. She would have to be careful from now on. Her words were meant as a warning to Malcolm. If he was up to anything, pretending to be helping her, but doing the opposite, she would soon find out.

They had reached the street where Heather's

house was located. Perhaps she should confront him now. It was as good a time as any. She would lead him into discussion of the lock, and why he had said he had broken it, when he had not.

But Malcolm's mind was on something else, and it was he who spoke. "Do you know what I think? I think we ought to take a look at that old wardrobe. You did say the noises seemed to come directly from it. Let's see if we can't get past that tight-lipped duenna who runs your house and do a little investigating."

Heather couldn't help laughing nervously. "Celine's out," she said. "I didn't even get a chance to—" She stopped in mid sentence. She had been going to say, *to ask her about last night*. But she didn't want to put Malcolm on his guard by mentioning last night. She would go along with him, to "investigate" the old wardrobe. She would watch him with great care. Perhaps he would make a slip. Then she might be able to figure out what he was up to. . . .

"You didn't get a chance to what?" Malcolm asked as Heather fumbled in her handbag for the key to the front door.

"To . . . to find out where she was going. But she's gone for the day. She told me she took one off every now and then. And she left me a cryptic note, written this morning." Heather fitted the key in the lock. "So we have complete freedom. She won't be around to look askance when we troop up to the bedroom."

Malcolm tried to look wicked. "Are you sure you feel safe?"

"Of course," Heather said lightly. "I'm Sherlock and you're Watson, remember?"

Malcolm persisted as they climbed the staircase

to the second floor. "Ah, yes, but Sherlock Holmes did not possess dark shining locks, nor tilted green eyes. He definitely wasn't pretty, and then there's the fact he was a man. . . ."

Heather looked around at him. "I just *know* you're an absolute gentleman, Malcolm—" Without warning the bantering was cut short. Heather's shoe had caught on something and she lost her balance. Her body twisted sharply and she fell backward into Malcolm's arms. He caught her securely, but they teetered for a moment, a tangle of arms and legs on the steep staircase. At last they steadied themselves, and Malcolm grinned rudely at her.

"See? You *do* care."

Confused, Heather bent over to retrieve her shoe. She used the few seconds to recover from the shock that had run through her when she fell against Malcolm's chest, clutching at him for support. For she had distinctly felt a holster, tucked out of sight and close to his body beneath his jacket.

Malcolm was carrying a gun!

She forced herself to stand upright, to smile at him. "Malcolm, don't be an ass," she said. "Well, I knew I should have had those old carpet tacks pulled out. Come on." She hurried up the few remaining steps, her mind racing. A gun! She had been right to suspect Malcolm. His friendliness and curiosity hid some other purpose—something sinister. And now she was alone in this house with him. If he had been the intruder last night, had left her locked in the old house in the dark, what would he try to do with her now? Cold fear clutched at her.

"I'm glad you didn't get them fixed, you know,"

Malcolm was saying. "How else would I have got to hold you?" He was so happy in his little charade, he didn't notice her rising panic! She fought desperately for self-control. At all costs, she mustn't let him know what she had discovered about him.

Briskly she led the way to the main bedroom. Malcolm immediately swung the doors of the ancient armoire wide. He inspected the interior for several minutes, knocking at the wooden panels, and staring closely at the sides and upper shelves. At last he stood back. "No treasure, no skeletons, no secret panels. Just a musty old closet." He shrugged and turned to her. "But quite a museum piece, don't you think? Those old-time woodworkers really knew their stuff, all right."

He shut the doors again, and examined them closely. Then he stepped into the small space along the wall by the huge armoire and gave it a little shove from the side. "Must weigh a ton," he grunted.

Brushing his hands, he stood once again in front of the glowering old armoire, looking thoughtful. "I've got an idea," he said at last. "There's something I want to try. Here, you get inside." He took her arm and steered her toward the armoire. He opened the doors again.

"Get inside? What for?"

"You'll see. Come on."

"Malcolm, I—I don't want to get inside."

"Don't be ridiculous. You have to. I'm too big."

"Malcolm, no—"

"You told me you weren't a sissy, Heather. Now stop being silly. You'll spoil everything." And he took her very firmly under the arms and actually lifted her into the wardrobe. Then, loudly and very firmly, he slammed the doors shut.

In the sudden blackness, cut off from all light and sanity, Heather began to scream. *"No, Malcolm, you can't do this—no!"* She began to pound at the doors, begging for release from this stifling prison, this trap.

The doors gave way, and Heather tumbled out. She was sobbing as Malcolm drew her to her feet. The words came breathlessly. "I don't know what you want, Malcolm. I don't know who you are, but you won't get away with this. You can't!"

He shook her roughly. "Can't what, Heather? What is it? What in God's name is wrong?"

Heather's head seemed to clear a little and she focused on him. He was staring at her, his face ashen. Taking a deep breath, she spoke deliberately. "You can't deny it, not now. *You* were the one who locked me inside the old house last night!"

"Locked you inside the old house?" Alarm spread across his features.

"Yes, and I was stuck there all night, you'll be happy to know. And it could only have been you, because you were the one who so mysteriously got the door open without a key. I don't know how you did it. And you were the one who was prowling around that very first day, doing 'research' as you called it, and now you're carrying that *gun*—"

"Wait a minute, wait a minute. Start again. Somebody locked you inside the old house last night? What were you doing there?"

"I heard noises again. I went down to investigate—"

"All alone?"

"Of course all alone. But you must know that, you must have seen me."

Malcolm frowned. "I didn't see you," he said

shortly and turned away. He paced back and forth a few times, then stared out the window. Heather could think of nothing to say. This was a new Malcolm. He had lost his air of cheerful good humor. He frightened her.

Squaring his shoulders, he turned to face her. "Somebody has started to play rough," he said grimly. "I can see I can't keep you out of it any longer. It looks as if I'm going to have to tell you a few things about myself. But I'm relying on you, Heather. You must not let anyone else know."

Heather stared at him dubiously. "Know what?"

He let out a long breath. "That I'm not a writer. . . ."

"I figured that one out for myself," Heather said dryly. "What are you, then?"

"I'm a cop. I'm undercover, doing some work for Interpol."

Heather was dumbfounded. "A—a cop? she breathed.

"Yes; for the last year or so. Want to see my identification?"

"No . . ." she said awkwardly, "it's all right."

"Look, I'm not at liberty to explain it all. But I can tell you that we've been trying to get our hands on a ring of thieves—highly accomplished thieves who specialize in art and jewelry. They've been operating practically unchecked all over Europe. We've traced their main movements to Switzerland. They like it here—lots of rich foreigners in the resort towns . . . Gstaad, St. Moritz. They can hide their profits in numbered Swiss bank accounts. Besides, Switzerland is close to everything . . . Italy, France, Austria.

"We know who some of these people are. And one of them, at least has been associated with this town. But there's a kingpin somewhere, a big brain behind it all. We haven't moved in on any of the little guys yet, because we want to get the big fish. That's my job; that's why I'm here."

"That's why you're here? Here in this house?" Heather asked, trying to absorb what he was saying.

"Yes. You see, they've got to have some sort of headquarters. We can't figure it out yet. This place came under scrutiny, naturally. . . ." He looked as if he didn't want to continue.

"Naturally? Why? Just because we've got a spooky old place next door—Anyway, we looked inside. You saw for yourself that no one's been in there for years."

"So it would seem," Malcolm agreed.

"But it's so hard to believe," cried Heather.

"I know that. It puts everyone under suspicion. Like that housekeeper of yours. She *is* a strange cookie. . . ."

"And who else?"

"We're very careful; we're looking at people with large, unexplained incomes . . . people with isolated homes who might do this sort of thing."

"And you thought the noises in my house might have something to do with it all?"

"Everything's worth checking out."

"But you've been so helpful. Was it just so you could look this place over?" Heather persisted.

Malcolm looked acutely uncomfortable. "No," he said, "that wasn't all of it. You yourself came under considerable suspicion."

Heather was astonished: "But why?"

"Because of—associations you had." Malcolm's cheeks reddened. "Look, I don't think we should go any further with this. I've found out enough about you now to trust you. I have to let you know this much because somebody is obviously checking our movements out closely."

"Wait a minute. What association of mine are you talking about, Malcolm?"

"I'm not happy to be the one to tell you this . . . ."

"Go on."

He paced out another tight circle. "Frederic."

"Frederic? I don't understand. . . ."

"Your fiancé was under observation for some months before he died, Heather. We knew him to be deeply involved with this ring."

"It can't be true!" Images of Frederic came rushing into Heather's consciousness. Frederic smiling, sure of himself, always on the move, beautifully dressed, and with impeccable manners . . . . Heather's hands clenched into tight fists. "No! You can't make me believe it!"

Malcolm spoke quietly. "I can give you proof, if you like."

Now it was Heather who paced around the room. "But it's crazy. He never—he wouldn't do anything like that!"

"But how well did you know him?" Malcolm persisted gently. He spent most of his time traveling; you saw him seldom enough when you were in the States. . . ."

"I know, I know. But he was well-known. He was an art dealer. He had to see a lot of people, go to auctions. . . . We would have been together once we were married. . . ." Heather's voice trailed off. It *was* possible. He did know all the right people; that would be a help, if he were dealing in stolen pieces. Frederic . . . always smooth, sophisticated. "But how could he be a thief?"

"He didn't commit the thefts. He was involved in

selling the stolen goods, and moving them from country to country. He knew rich collectors, people who asked few questions if they wanted an object or a painting badly enough. There are lots of ways to disguise a stolen work, especially if much of what you are moving *is* legitimate."

Impulsively, Heather picked up the little photograph of Frederic that she kept on her bedside table. She thrust it at Malcolm. "*This* is Frederic. Frederic Brandon. *My* Frederic. Are we talking about the same man?"

"I'm afraid so." Malcolm's brow was creased in apology.

Heather stared at the photo as if hypnotized. It seemed that she was looking at a stranger's face. Could she have really loved him, this handsome man, now so alien? The smile seemed cold now, cold with more than the distance of death. . . . Her fond memories of him shifted out of focus. With a sick new sensation of betrayal, she flung the picture down. How could she have realized so little about him?

Malcolm hovered awkwardly near her, trying to soften the terrible news. He fumbled for words. "I'd hoped . . . never to have to tell you," he said. "But I'm worried now. There's danger, especially if there was an intruder last night."

"Do you mean danger from the others—the people in Frederic's ring?"

"Yes, I do. They're watching us. They knew we were inside the old house. They must have known the boards had been removed."

"How did you open that door, anyway?" Heather demanded.

"I picked the lock. Elementary skill for a detective."

"That made me suspicious of you—though I didn't know exactly what you were after. I thought it was *you* in the old house last night, Malcolm!"

Malcolm looked very seriously at her. "It was not me. And I would like very much to know who it was. I have a feeling that this house, somehow, does contain the key to everything. If I could just get a handle on whatever that key is—that link—"

Abruptly Malcolm whirled around. His eyes flew to the bedroom doorway.

Heather followed his gaze. Her stomach tightened painfully.

Celine was standing in the doorway. She was absolutely motionless, and Heather had a flickering image of some predator, watching . . . tense, stealthy, biding its time. How long had she been there, listening to them?

Celine's expression was faintly contemptuous as she spoke. "I heard voices, miss. I came to tell you I'm home."

Chapter 7

Malcolm and Heather stared at the door after Celine had left.

"Good Lord. That woman gives me the willies," Malcolm whispered, his face a mask of comical alarm. "Do you think she overheard much?"

"It's impossible to tell," Heather sighed.

"She's like a stone statue—a medieval Sybil. One of the witches they used to burn around here."

Heather laughed. "Maybe you should have been a writer, Malcolm. You've got a picturesque imagination."

"It could be bad for us if she did overhear—if she's involved," he said soberly. "'I've got them running a check on her back at headquarters. It'll be interesting to hear what they turn up."

"I'm curious myself. Aunt Rachel never told us much about her."

"Well, we'd better talk somewhere else. I can't risk breaking my cover again. Things look bad enough with these prowlers snooping at night."

"Just tell me one thing, Malcolm. Why on earth did you shut me in the wardrobe like that?"

Malcolm looked sheepish. "Honestly, if I'd known about your horrors last night, I'd never have done it. It was kind of dumb, but I wanted you to go in there and make a few little noises, just to see how they sounded from the outside. Here. I'll climb in, and you listen."

Heather was dubious, but she helped him squeeze inside, and carefully shut the doors of the wardrobe. He scuffled and thumped and muttered. The noises were mysterious enough, but they lacked the muffled, tentative, floating quality of the ones she had heard in the night.

She swung the doors open. "Nope. Nothing like it." Malcolm unfolded himself and clambered out awkwardly.

"Whew! I know how you must have felt, sealed into that tomb next door for hours. I'd like to catch the person who did that. Is it locked now?"

"I banged a few nails in this morning. Not that that would stop anyone."

"It'll do for now. Come on. We're getting out of here. You need a rest from this place."

Celine was drifting silently around in her kitchen. She didn't look up when Malcolm announced that Heather wouldn't be home for dinner. When they got out to the street, Heather experienced an enormous sense of relief. She drew a deep breath of the fragrant, late-afternoon air.

"I know a place where we can get some superb raclette, if you're in the mood. You barely touched your lunch."

Gratefully, Heather allowed him to direct her to a restaurant several blocks away. The tumultuous events of the past twenty-four hours had left her numb and drained. They found a booth in a secluded corner, and sat in a companionable silence for several minutes. Malcolm ordered wine, and Heather sipped it, her hand trembling.

She spoke thoughtfully. "I can't absorb it all. Frederic—a criminal . . . ."

He watched her sympathetically. "Perhaps . . . perhaps you would have found out in some other way. It could have been in a worse way than this. Maybe it'll be better for you, in the long run."

"I suppose it was natural enough for you to suspect me, since I was close to him," she said tentatively.

Malcolm spoke in a low, guarded voice. "I got a call from Paris, suggesting I keep an eye on you. I'm afraid they'd been trailing the two of you. They were assuming you'd know something."

"It's strange," Heather said, not really listening to him. "I was always a little amazed that Frederic would choose me, a wide-eyed innocent, when he could have had almost any woman. All those laughing creatures who always knew what to say, who had been everywhere, who knew how to dress. . . ."

"Perhaps, underneath it all, he really did appreciate the finer things in life. No one could hold a candle to you, you know," said Malcolm shyly.

Heather lowered her eyes. "He was just so—sort of dashing. He could make me feel important and somehow beautiful. . . ."

"You *are* beautiful. That first time I crashed into you I thought so. And when I connected you to the name sent from Interpol my heart sank. I didn't want you to be involved with those crooks. And I'm glad you're really not."

Heather smiled. "And I'm glad *you're* not the sinister figure I'd imagined you were. But a *detective*? You don't really look the part, you know."

"That's the story of my success. What did you expect—a scruffy raincoat, maybe?"

"Your scholarly cover is very suitable, really. But I'd drop that tale about being a detective writer. Anyone could see through that if I could."

Malcolm grinned. "It's been useful, at times. Lets me hobnob with uniformed cops, and be seen trotting into the local police station."

"Somehow I don't imagine a Scotsman being connected with the mysterious Interpol."

"Well, it's an international organization, so of course it attracts all sorts. The less we fit the stereotype of undercover cops, the better."

Heather was thoughtful again. "I'm just terribly confused. It seems the past few days, since I arrived in Sion, have been the most crazy, eventful ones ever. It's all helter-skelter, as if the world has tipped one degree too far on its axis. Nobody, but nobody, is who he seems to be."

"I wonder if that includes the glamorous Geraldine," mused Malcolm.

"Geraldine? Yes, she's been going around without telling anyone about that husband of hers, Anton Valdemar. She doesn't use his name. The fact that she's married at all was another little shock to me."

"What does she call herself? I'll run her through records."

"Do you know, I can't for the life of me remember. I thought about it before. It's a rather common French surname, I think."

"Easy enough to find out. Don't worry about it," he told her reassuringly. "You're not eating your dinner. Come on, you need it."

Thank God for Malcolm, Heather thought warmly. His square face was comforting, friendly. And the little restaurant had the same feeling about it. Heather tried to give herself over to the joys of raclette. But the hearty cheese dish—even as beautifully prepared as this one—was too much for her. She put her fork down again. She struggled to bring some order to the thoughts that tumbled through her mind. Frederic . . . Geraldine . . . Interpol. Noises and prowlers in the night. Did any of this have anything to do with Aunt Rachel, with that sad fragment of a letter—a letter that took too long to reach its destination?

"You're doing it again," said Malcolm gently. "What are you thinking about now?"

"I'm thinking . . . about Aunt Rachel, I'm afraid. What's the connection with those noises? I—I can't help wondering if she wasn't scared to death. Her heart was so bad. . . ."

Malcolm reached out and touched her hand. "The more the action seems to swirl around that house, the more I'm beginning to share your fears. But we can't jump to conclusions. So far, there's just no way we can tie the factors together. There's no concrete connection between those crooks and your house."

"Not even through Celine?"

"Not yet," he said, taking his hand away and dabbing at his mouth with a napkin. "I'm not satisfied at all. It's just an empty house, as far as I can see. There may be something in the noises, some freaky distortion of things from another source. But it beats me what it could be. I'm working on it. Don't worry." He pondered for a moment. "Tell me more about this guy last night. What did you hear or see? Exactly what happened?"

Heather told him, as completely as she could remember.

He scowled as she finished her story. "And you

had to sit there all night, scared out of your wits? Dammit, I'm going to get that guy—"

"I can't be sure it was a man, Malcolm. I couldn't see a thing."

"But what woman would pull a trick like that? Celine?"

"It hardly seems possible. Or that's what I thought." Heather shrugged.

"Still, with those eyes of hers, maybe she can see in the dark—like a cat. They say witches used to change at will into the forms of their familiars. . . ."

Heather shuddered. "Will you stop mentioning witches? I won't be able to go back to my house to sleep tonight. Besides, there's no cat around the place. That I'm sure of. If she *is* a witch, she's a modern one."

"Probably has a jet-powered broom," grinned Malcolm.

Heather couldn't help smiling back.

"There," he said. "That's better. We've got to stop being gloomy about all this."

Heather brightened. "Yes. Let's be practical. What are we going to do next?"

Malcolm's brows shot up. "What are *we* going to do? What am I going to do, you mean. This is my job, and I'm not going to let you get into any more trouble over it."

"Malcolm, I'm already into it up to my neck."

"Hmm . . . so you are. Well, it can't hurt to tell you a little more about what *I'm* going to do. Part of the problem, as I told you, is finding out who the ringleader of all this is. That's the big mystery. It's somebody very clever indeed, and we haven't got a line on him. I'll have to watch all the characters—Celine, probably, maybe Geraldine, and some you don't know about. That guy with her at lunch looked faintly familiar. But the idea is to keep them off guard. They have to think they're safe. So if they've seen me with you, and know we've been snooping around, they can't be allowed to suspect who I am. Do you think you can handle the skulduggery?"

"Sure. What do I have to do, just act natural around Celine?"

"If that's possible. She's given off waves of disapproval often enough. There's little doubt she thinks we're lovers. Would it be too difficult to let her go on thinking that?"

Heather blushed. "No, of course not."

"And be friendly to Geraldine if ever she condescends to nod at you again."

"That'll be harder," said Heather with a grimace.

"We'll just let on we're two happy young people, without a care in the world. We'll be cheerful and exceedingly dumb. It'll work out well, because I want to keep an eye on you to keep you out of harm's way." His gaze held her eyes for a moment. His expression was so earnest that Heather laughed gently.

"Malcolm, I'm a big girl. I can take care of myself."

"You don't fully understand who we're fooling around with," he said very sternly. "These guys are *big*. They manage to move stuff successfully all over the map. None of the regular customs techniques ever seem to trip them up. They ship jewels around as if they were postcards."

"Jewels? I thought they were into art."

"They are—jewels, too. They scramble into hotels in the big resort towns. Movie stars, people like that—they insist on taking their diamonds with them to the ski slopes. The thieves break them out of their settings, and they turn up later, thousands of miles away, gracing some other ivory throat. Vanity, greed—what is it? But somehow there's always a ready market for hot gems. Especially diamonds."

"I read not long ago about a big robbery in a hotel in St. Moritz. A tycoon's wife, or an Arab, something like that. Wasn't it a necklace that was stolen?"

"Yes, and mighty big stones, too. We're very interested in those. The Mogul Stars, they're called. Disappeared off the face of the earth. But only for a while. Whoever took them has to get them out of Switzerland. Maybe to have them reset in Italy. Or recut in Amsterdam. They haven't turned up yet. We're pretty sure they're still here. And the trail, faint as it is, leads to Sion." He straightened up in his seat. "But that's all I can tell you about *that*. In fact, I've already told you too much, young lady. I can't think what's come over me." He took a long gulp of his wine.

"Malcolm, don't worry, please. I'll help you if I can. You haven't been indiscreet. Maybe I can do things you can't reasonably do. Keep an eye on Geraldine, for instance. . . ."

"I can handle it, I told you. It's far too dangerous. I mean it." He ordered cognac for them both. "A bracer to steel your nerves for the haunted house. You're to sleep tonight, and sleep well. No forays into the dark, promise?"

"Oh, I'm tired enough to sleep, I think. But I'm in this whether you like it or not, you know. I have a lot of questions to clear up concerning Aunt Rachel."

Malcolm sighed. "I can see you've made up your mind, all right. But there isn't much you can do."

"Well, what about Geraldine? I mean, she was—associated with Frederic."

"I told you, she's on my list."

Something clicked in Heather's mind. "What about her husband, Anton Valdemar?"

Malcolm rolled his eyes to the ceiling. "Oh, no," he groaned. "You've lucked onto it. All right. I've been making inquiries about him ever since we saw that nice, isolated setup in the mountains. But I'm telling you, it's top secret. A wrong move—a wrong *word* even—could wreck things. You've got to understand that." He sighed loudly. "What have I done?"

But Heather was paying him no attention. Her mind was racing ahead. "He fits the bill, you know. Lots of money, they say. Where does it come from?"

"We don't know, yet," Malcolm said reluctantly.

"And he's married to *her*—that's enough, right there."

"Right."

"He bears watching," Heather said, a gleam in her eye.

"I'm watching him, I told you."

"I've met him. He's so strange . . . sort of fierce and secretive. But when he was with those children, he was so totally different! I know he *cares* about those children."

Malcolm glowered impatiently. "Nobody's accusing him of anything—yet. In fact, I want you to stop thinking about it, stop speculating. Even that could be dangerous at this point."

"Malcolm, I've got an idea. When I was at the clinic he said that he was short of help. What if I went there to volunteer? I've had some fieldwork with children in college, and—"

"*No!*" Malcolm exploded, so loudly that a few

startled diners turned to stare. He hunched his shoulders and lowered his voice. "That's not a good idea. Not a good idea at all. Do you hear?"

"It's legitimate anyway," Heather said eagerly. "I can do it on my own, even if you don't approve. You can't stop me."

Malcolm fought to suppress his agitation. "It's risky, I tell you. You'd be way up there, twenty miles from town, cut off from my help if anything happened—and if we're right, he's a dangerous man. That's not to say that we have anything to go on, by the way. It's just a stab in the dark."

"From the sound of things, it's as good a guess as any, right now," Heather said triumphantly. "And I'm going to do it. He was offhand about Aunt Rachel, I thought. Too offhand. Don't you think it's just a little bit of a coincidence that he happened to be her physician at the time of her death?"

"No," said Malcolm angrily. "We've got too many coincidences as it is."

"Well, I want to find out more about Aunt Rachel. Nothing will stop me from doing that. Interpol might as well not exist as far as I'm concerned. But I won't interfere with anything, I promise."

"I'd call it maximum interference," Malcolm said sulkily.

"No, it isn't. You're just being gallant. You think you're protecting me, but I don't need protection. I need answers. Now, the first thing I'll do is find out what I can around town about him. . . ."

"You can't go around asking obvious questions. That's just exactly what you can't do," said Malcolm through his teeth. "You'll blow the whole thing."

"I won't go around asking questions. I'll just ask Oscar."

"Who's Oscar?"

"He's an old man, a toymaker I knew when I was child here. He's been around forever, and he knows everyone. I promised to have him to tea. Celine drove him from our house it seems, in the same way she managed to cut Aunt Rachel off from all her old friends. He was hurt, and I promised to make it up to him. I'll get rid of Celine tomorrow afternoon."

"And how are you going to be subtle about that?" Malcolm looked dreadfully unhappy.

"I'll find a way. I'm as good at plotting as the next person."

"What do you expect to find out from this Oscar?"

"Just things—where Anton Valdemar is from, how long his clinic has been there."

"Won't he object to being grilled over his tea?"

"Nonsense. He loves to talk. And he has a wonderful memory. Besides, I'm very fond of him. I really do want to try to make him feel better about losing Aunt Rachel as a friend. Even if I learn nothing at all, it will be an afternoon well spent. But he knows Dr. Valdemar. They were together in Oscar's toy shop when I went in the other day." She smiled brightly at Malcolm. "Cheer up. It certainly can't hurt. And I won't get out of line, I promise."

"You had better not. I'm more than serious about that." Malcolm waved for the check. He looked so troubled that Heather felt a little guilty. But she had made up her mind. She would prove to him that she could help.

"Don't worry, Malcolm. I know how secret your work is. You must believe that. I won't take a step without consulting you first. Okay?"

He didn't appear to be soothed in the least. As

they walked home in the falling dusk he stared down at his feet, saying nothing. He left her at the door, and turned to go without speaking. Then he seemed to think better of it. He came back to her, and stood silently for a moment. "All right," he whispered at last. "But I never should have let you in on all this. When I decided that you weren't part of it, I was so relieved . . . I've behaved unprofessionally. I guess I'm still new at this game but they could have my badge."

"You trusted me, Malcolm. You have to trust people sometimes. And you were right." Impulsively, she squeezed both his hands.

The anxiety in his eyes was real. "Please be careful. Don't do anything at all without consulting me." He returned the pressure of her hands for a moment, and then he was gone.

Heather slipped quietly into the house and upstairs. She did not encounter Celine, for which she thanked some kindly star as she prepared for bed. The whirling confusion of her thoughts had settled into one orderly, simple vein. She was in control now. This time she would do something to actively solve the events that haunted this silent old house.

She sank into the comfort of her bed, and fell into a serene, uninterrupted sleep.

THE NEXT MORNING, still feeling calm and certain of her actions, she made up a detailed and very specific list of errands for Celine. She managed an arch little smile as she gave the woman the list. "Malcolm is coming this afternoon," she said sweetly. "You can have some time off—if you'd like. Perhaps there's a movie you'd like to see?"

Celine's gaze flickered knowingly. "Yes, of course. Why not a movie?"

When Celine had gone, Heather telephoned Oscar's shop.

"Tea? Why that would be fine, but . . . ." The old man's voice faltered.

"Mrs. Dumas is out for the day," Heather said cheerfully.

She heard his chuckle at the other end of the line. "That's something of a relief, yes. All right, I'll come."

At the appointed hour, he stood at the door, doffing his hat.

"Oscar, welcome to this house again," Heather said, showing him into the sunny kitchen.

"Nothing has changed at all," he said, looking around him with an air of vast pleasure. "How well I remember the afternoons I spent chatting with Rachel Savorin at this very table," he said. "I only wish I had seen her, before . . . . It's good of you to invite me here. This house holds many enjoyable memories, Miss Ashley."

"Call me Heather. You always did when I was a little girl."

"Heather, then."

"Sit down, please. I'll just get the kettle. There are cakes and things. . . ."

Oscar helped himself to a petit four. "I'll say one thing for that woman. She does cook well," he remarked approvingly, smacking his lips. "I think I'll have another. How she would scowl if she knew Oscar Caron was here in her kitchen, enjoying the fruits of her labors. Well, it's a strange world, and no mistake about it."

He settled comfortably into the old rocker that

sat at one end of the table. Heather took a chair near him.

"I wanted you to come, Oscar, for that very reason. Because she's kept you away, and it isn't right. Perhaps we won't have to worry about her in the near future, and I hope you'll come anytime you like."

"Oh. She is leaving your employ?"

"Not immediately. But she's as unpleasant as you described. . . . I don't like to let the woman go simply because of her—what shall I say—manners? She might need the money, after all. Where did you say she was from? Not from around here or in the Valais?"

Oscar waved a hand vaguely. "Oh, I'm not sure. Possibly Vaud, or the Grisons. One doesn't bother to find these things out. . . ."

Heather laughed. "Not when a person doesn't encourage it."

"Right you are. Why, I know everyone in this town, I imagine. Most of them are ordinary people, a little good in them, a little not so good. When you get to be my age, you know that well enough. But now and then," he said, waving an emphatic forefinger, "you meet one like *that!*" His eyes twinkled cheerfully as he made short work of another petit four.

"It must be marvelous," Heather said, to be like you . . . to be so well-liked in Sion. It's a beautiful town. You must have seen many changes."

"Sion changes, but she's ancient, you know. A lot remains the same."

"Like the cathedral, the guildhall . . . ."

"And this old house," nodded Oscar.

"But there are new things. Those apartments on the edge of town for example."

"Some of us aren't fond of those. I say, let them

build. People are too fussy these days about 'preserving' old things, as they call it. I say, the new must come. It's a good thing for some." He smiled broadly. "Children live in those apartment buildings. Children for Oscar's toys. So it's good for me."

"You have a practical turn of mind," Heather laughed. Then she said quickly, "I saw some children the other day, with that man—Dr. Valdemar was it—you introduced me to him in your shop. He has a new place, a clinic, in the mountains at Ferpècle."

"Oh, yes, yes. He has a clinic up there. For the air. The children are sick with their lungs. Dr. Valdemar takes some sort of special interest in them. He's not a talkative man, that one, but some people admire him very much for his work."

"It must have taken a great deal of money to build such a place. It's very beautiful."

"Yes, they say he has a good deal of money." Oscar didn't elaborate, and Heather couldn't think of a way to further this line of inquiry without becoming obviously snoopy. She took another tack.

"I wonder what it is about the children's lungs. They were all so small, so fragile. It seems a shame that they're sick."

"It's the wheezing . . . the asthma, I think you say. The mountain air is good for them. We often have that sort of place for cures in Switzerland, as you know."

"It's a shame," Heather said. "More tea?"

"Oh, of course, yes." Oscar extended his cup. "Valdemar's an odd sort of fellow. Came here maybe five or six years ago. No, seven. He had his practice in town, you know. That's how I know him. A good doctor."

"He tended Aunt Rachel, for her heart."

"Is that so? I thought she was old Mazarell's patient. But then Mazarell was ill, wasn't he? Valdemar helped out for a while. But now they say he spends all his time up in the mountains. You wouldn't think it to see him, he's so gloomy all the time, but one hears that he's wonderful with these young ones."

"I wonder why he's so glum all the time," Heather began, watching Oscar closely.

"Must have something to do with that wife of his. She never behaved as a woman should. Went off years ago to see the sights, and only came back for the money now and then. Took the child, too."

"The child?"

"He has a little daughter. Wanted to keep her himself, I understand. But her mother hung on. Wouldn't give her up. Maybe that's natural for most mothers . . . but I don't know about this one. I just don't know."

"What was she like?" Heather asked, hoping her voice did not betray more than casual interest.

Oscar shifted in his chair. "Oh, I never really knew much about that one. Just a girl from out of town. That's all you could say about her. But here I am, old Oscar, gossiping about local things. You must tell me more about yourself, Heather. What you've been doing all these years, things like that." He smiled encouragingly at her and sipped his tea.

Heather drew a deep breath. "Well, there's not much to tell. I've been to university in the States. I haven't finished. I may go back."

"And how is your mama?"

"She was ill a few months back. That was why we didn't come when Aunt Rachel was sick. . . . But now mother is fine."

"I was sorry to hear that your father had died."

"We've got over that now, if you ever get over such things." Heather fiddled a little with one of the small cakes. She tried to think of some way to turn the conversation away from herself and back to the affairs of Anton Valdemar.

"And who is this young man you are seeing?" Oscar asked suddenly.

Heather looked at him in surprise.

"Ah, I see you are blushing." He nodded slyly. "Nothing escapes old Oscar, you know. I have to look after you, now that there is no one else here to do so. Now, you must confess. You have been seen by all the old gossips of Sion."

"His—his name is Malcolm McBride. Perhaps you've heard of him? He writes books. Detective stories."

"Detective stories? But that must be very interesting indeed. You are serious about him?"

"Oh, hardly. I've only just met him."

"Where does he come from with a name like that? McBride?"

"It's Scottish."

Oscar persisted, pleased with himself. "I've caught you out, I can tell. Is that all he does? Does one make a decent living out of writing these books?"

Heather tried to look stern. "I'm not *that* interested in him. I don't care how much money he makes, Oscar."

Oscar was earnestly paternal. "A young lady has to be very careful these days. What do you know about him, after all? He just turns up in town and sweeps you off your feet. . . ."

Heather chuckled at the thought. "I like him. He's very nice, really."

"And you are fairly well-off yourself with this house, you know. Young men have been known to take advantage of these things."

"Oscar, you're an old dear. But I haven't been swept off my feet."

Oscar looked mollified. He changed the subject. "Yes, it's a wonderful old house. Do you think you will stay here, to live? Or might you sell it?"

"I might, I suppose. I haven't thought about it yet."

"Well, whatever. You could make a good profit, I can tell you that."

"I expect it's considered historical. Malcolm tells me the old part—the section next door that we don't use at all, goes back to the fifteenth century."

"He knows that, does he?"

"Yes," said Heather quietly. "He—he also does historical research."

Oscar waved expansively. "Now that's interesting. There are plenty of tales to tell about all these old places in this part of Switzerland . . . about the goings-on during the religious struggles, the bitter wars between the Calvinists and the bishops."

"Yes," said Heather, eager to paint a false picture of Malcolm for the old man's benefit. "Malcolm is very interested in all that. He's even looking up the plans of some of the old buildings around here."

Oscar gave her an alert nod. "Very worthy. Very worthy. I can see he will amount to something after all, this young fellow of yours . . . . But it's getting late. I must go back to my store now. I'm enjoying our visit, of course, but you understand. . . ."

"Oh, I do understand. I'm glad you could come, even for a little while."

Oscar bowed. "And I am happy that this fine house has a mistress once again."

Heather escorted him to the door and watched him shamble off up the street. Her feelings were mixed. It had been good to see him, but the interview hadn't accomplished much. How did real investigators manage such things, she wondered.

But no doubt it was best to be careful. The important thing was not to tip her hand. Not to anyone. Malcolm's work was too important and too dangerous to risk that. At least Oscar hadn't sensed anything strange about her questions.

She knew what she would report to Malcolm. It was a case of so far so good. She shut the door and went back to the kitchen to clear up the tea things.

Chapter 8

Anton Valdemar seemed surprised at Heather's offer to work in the clinic on a volunteer basis. "You don't strike me as the sort of young woman who would be interested in such work," he said, swiveling around in his chair to stare thoughtfully out at the mountains.

Heather had rehearsed her little speech all the way up from Sion. She hadn't quite anticipated this response, but she was determined to convince him. "Oh, but you're not aware of my background, Dr. Valdemar."

He turned back to her. "I only know that you are the niece of a wealthy American woman, and that you've come to Sion because you inherited her house. It's true, of course, that you were curious about her death. . . ."

Heather bristled at his tone. "Our side of the family did as much as circumstances permitted to help Aunt Rachel. And if she was wealthy it doesn't necessarily follow that we ourselves are— nor that money, if we possessed it, would make us wicked."

He gave her a wintry smile. "A point well taken."

Heather plunged on. "I was referring to my professional background. I'm still a student, but I've done fieldwork in children's hospitals on my vacations. You see, I majored in child psychology at Boston University."

"And you have cut your studies short to come to Switzerland?"

"For various reasons, yes—I've decided to take the last couple of semesters off. But you can see, it's important to me to keep in touch with practical work in my field. When you remarked the other day that you were short-staffed here at the clinic, it started me thinking. At the moment, I don't need money, and I do have experience with children. If I were able to help out here, it would be beneficial to us both."

Anton Valdemar steepled his long fingers and stared into space. Heather couldn't help noticing his ruggedly carved profile, and the way his brows knitted in thought. He was an extremely attractive man, she admitted. There was an air about him of tenseness, of powerful inner forces held rigidly in check. . . .

"The children here are all severely asthmatic," he said at length. "I suppose you know that although the condition has some physiological basis, mostly to do with allergy, it is often severely complicated by psychological factors."

Heather nodded in agreement, but he continued to look through his fingers toward a space somewhere behind her. "The fact that you have training in child psychology . . . ." He paused, and Heather fought an impatient urge to finish his sentence for him.

The hands were suddenly placed flat on the desk in a gesture of decision. "All right, Miss Ashley. We'll try it out. I need help badly, but I am not willing to take on just anyone, be they volunteer or not. So we'll have to call it a probationary period. Does that meet with your approval?"

"Absolutely," said Heather, doing her best to appear cool and professional. Inside she was bubbling with elation. Wait until Malcolm heard about this! She smiled graciously at the doctor. "I can start anytime you like."

"It's hard work, you know."

"I know that very well. The children I've worked with were often emotionally disturbed or retarded. I know how powerful their needs can be. We were exposed to many—"

He raised his hand. "All right, you've convinced me. We'll see how it works out. You can start tomorrow."

Heather hummed to herself all the way down the valley and back into town. It had been a day of significant accomplishment. First the interview with Oscar—well-executed if inconclusive—and now the successful launching of herself as undercover operative at Dr. Valdemar's clinic.

She acknowledged a tiny feeling of guilt; she had misrepresented herself, and if it should turn out that Anton Valdemar had nothing to do with the criminals Malcolm was after . . . . But she had also been truthful about her previous work with children, and about her continuing interest in them. In its own way, her new job was completely legitimate.

Still, she couldn't help feeling oddly nervous. She knew it wasn't entirely due to the "danger" Malcolm had talked about if the criminal ring should discover her mission, or find out who Malcolm was working for.

It had to do with the forceful personality of Anton Valdemar himself, with whatever he held so carefully in check inside him. Was it some anger, some terrible pain? Or was it cunning—the cunning of a man who could control a ring of international thieves? Who would, perhaps, falsify a death certificate?

SHE MET MALCOLM for dinner that evening. They chose another restaurant, and again sat at an isolated table, well away from other diners. Whenever the waiter approached, they were careful to talk lightly of nothing at all, the way they assumed young lovers would. But when they were certain they were alone, their heads were bent in conspiracy.

"I got the job!" was Heather's first announcement. Malcolm looked uncomfortable, but she ignored his reaction and hurried on to an excited description of her interview and its consequences.

Malcolm was relieved that she hadn't had to lie her way into a post at the clinic. You could easily be caught out by anyone who knew about these things professionally."

"That's the beauty of it," Heather said eagerly. "I didn't lie, and to a certain extent, anyway, I know what I'm doing around children with emotional problems. But I didn't get a lot of information out of Oscar in my other attempt to be a detective."

"The guy resisted you, did he?" Malcolm was doing his best not to look smug. A smile hovered at the corners of his mouth.

"Well, there wasn't that much for him to tell, I guess. He knew Anton Valdemar, but apparently more by reputation than anything else. He said very little that I didn't already know. In fact, he had a lot more to say about Celine than anyone else. . . ."

"Ah, that reminds me." Malcolm fairly glowed with eagerness. "Guess what headquarters tells me about our friend Celine?"

"Do you mean they've actually got something on her?"

"Yep. It's not new, mind you. Goes back more than twenty years, in fact."

"Come on, Malcolm, don't stall. What did you find out?"

"Celine, it seems, used to work in hotels and pensions in Switzerland and France—most often as a chambermaid, later as a housekeeper." Malcolm paused for dramatic effect. "Twenty-five years ago she was arrested and imprisoned for theft."

Heather was impressed. "Really? Oh, Malcolm, it all ties in!"

"Perhaps. . . . What did Oscar tell you about her?"

"He admitted he knows very little, in spite of the fact that he takes great pride in knowing absolutely everybody in town. He merely said she was one of a kind, and not worth getting to know."

"So she turned up in your great-aunt's employ about a year ago?"

"That's about right. She was new in town then. Oscar thinks she may have come from Vaud or the Grisons. She must have treated him shamefully, because he didn't want to discuss her much beyond that."

"Well, we draw a blank, then, for the years between. Not much we can do about it . . . unless you can apply your interrogation technique to the woman."

"I could, but she's about as talkative as a clam. Wait a minute! I just had a thought. She must have written to Aunt Rachel, applying for the job. And she probably supplied references. Surely that correspondence would be around somewhere. And what about the lawyers, the ones from the Savorin family, in Zurich? I could get in touch with them."

Malcolm's eyes twinkled. "I'm proud of you. Good ideas all."

"Thanks. I told you I'd be a big help."

"But be careful, Heather. I mean it." He shook a forefinger sternly for emphasis. "And watch it around this Dr. Valdemar. He's not some simple old craftsman like Oscar. For all we know, he's a dangerous man."

"Malcolm, you're just like a mother hen." But Heather felt a little nervous flutter in the pit of her stomach. In spite of her carefree façade she knew she would be approaching Anton Valdemar with caution and respect.

IN THE MORNING, the meadow in front of the glass-walled clinic was bright with dew. Heather, having arrived very early, took an impulsive romp through the grass. She didn't mind waiting until a more seemly hour, when everyone inside would be up, before beginning any serious work. Meanwhile there was delicious greeny-scented grass, and the moist cups of the flowers turned to the sky. . . .

This high, clean air must be wonderful for the children, she thought. They had an entire little valley to themselves to run and play and be free in without the terrible anxiety of their illness.

Heather had in fact seen children with asthma during her fieldwork in hospitals. They struggled horribly for breath until the staff could get the machine to them, the life-giving oxygen. The gasping was one of the most wrenching sounds Heather could imagine. Routinely, parents would panic over this. In turn, panicking increased the child's anxiety, making the attack worse. And so the vicious cycle would contine. That was why some children had to be separated from their families and sent to places such as this one. The separation was sad, but the illness was worse, Heather knew.

The sun was edging higher now, evaporating the crystal globes of dew that glimmered in the grass. Heather inhaled deeply. She was feeling energetic, sure of herself. She had slept well again last night, and had managed to maintain a façade of politeness with Celine. And she knew Malcolm would make sure she wasn't exposed to any unnecessary danger.

Still, she looked sharply from her contemplation of the meadow flowers when she felt someone was watching her. She gave a little gasp, and immediately felt foolish. It was only a child. A little dark-haired child of about five, with large solemn eyes.

This was the child she had seen clutching Anton Valdemar's hand in the bus. And, she suddenly remembered, the same one whose image smiled from a photograph on his desk. His daughter?

"Who are you?" Heather asked quietly.

The child stood very still, watching Heather in the dreamy, musing way some children do. Her eyes, brown and dark fringed, flickered away shyly at the sound of Heather's voice. Then cautiously she looked back. She put a finger or two into her mouth. But she didn't say a word.

Heather knew better than to rush up to the little girl and overwhelm her with attention. Instead, she turned back to what she had been doing. "I'm just checking these buttercups for dew," she said companionably. The child continued to watch her with interest. "Sometimes you find an ant in one, having a bath." The little girl took a step or two closer.

Heather held a buttercup up very close to her face, as if it were the most interesting thing in the world. The child began to look around herself for buttercups. There must be something to these everyday things, something she'd never thought of before. She picked one of her own.

"I haven't got an ant in *mine*," she said in a disappointed tone.

"Well, sometimes you have to pick several," Heather advised her. "Look, there's one!" Heather pointed and the child reached out a delicate hand.

A black and very swift little ant scurried across the petals of the flower and disappeared.

"Oh, dear," said Heather "I guess we've missed him."

"I guess he finished his bath," commented the little girl judiciously. Then she eyed Heather once again. "Do you live here?" she asked.

"No, not here. I've come to visit the place over there." She pointed to the clinic, its glass panels glinting in the morning sun.

"I live there," said the little girl.

"Then I've come to visit you," smiled Heather. "Why don't you tell me your name?"

"It's Susie," said the child, and then she was overcome with another gust of shyness. She skipped away, attempting to look unconcerned. Heather followed her toward the building, keeping a reassuring distance. Susie turned around and waved.

"Hurry up," she called.

Heather smiled to herself and quickened her pace. She was very close to the clinic before she realized that Anton Valdemar was standing at the top of the front steps watching her approach.

"I see you've met Susie," he said. "She's usually very shy with strangers."

"Well, we've just made friends," Heather replied a little breathlessly. "We were discussing the secret life of ants and flowers."

"Glad to hear it," Dr. Valdemar said. He took the little girl's hand. "This is my daughter, Susie."

"She already knows my name," whispered the child severely.

He looked down at her gravely. "Ah. I'm sorry. I should have realized. But we must show Miss Ashley around our place."

"Is *that* her name?" The child's eyes regarded her with alarm.

Heather laughed. "No, it isn't. I hope you and Dr. Valdemar will call me Heather."

"Yes," said the doctor, "we'll do that. And I suppose you should really call me Anton." He looked embarrassed. "I'm trying to reduce the 'hospital' atmosphere around here, anyway." He turned abruptly to lead the way inside.

They spent a long morning orienting Heather to the facilities at the clinic and to the children's various case histories. Her duties were rather undefined because Anton had never had help before—other than from the nurse, Mrs. Rykman, who was a widow and lived in at the clinic with the children; and a woman who came in from the village to cook and clean.

Heather was asked to help Mrs. Rykman and the doctor with the daily management of the children. Some required more attention than others. She could play with and supervise the children, and participate in their therapy if required.

She spent an hour or two going through files, reading about the backgrounds of the children. Curiously enough, a file had conscientiously been made up for Susie, detailing her family life—which was Anton Valdemar's own. Why would he have any need to refer to it?

Ethically, however, it was the correct thing for a doctor to do.

Heather was particularly interested in this file, along with one other—that of great-aunt Rachel, which she would try to get access to. She didn't wish to slip up on the very first day and be seen rummaging through the wrong file cabinet. There would be time for that later. Right now she was immersed in Dr. Valdemar's terse notes on the case history of one Susie Valdemar—his own daughter.

Susie had been born five years and two months ago here in Sion. She had been slightly delicate— nothing very serious—and her father had taken numerous measures, which he had carefully detailed, to build up her physical strength. She was making good progress. Then there was a brusque notation: "Age two years, four months: parents separated. Child removed from this physician's care by mother. Attempts made repeatedly at contact." Following that, there there were entries made at sporadic intervals during the past three years or so:

Child asthmatic. Custody dispute frustrating efforts of this physician to bring child to therapeutic mountain atmosphere. Evidence of neglect by mother. Unable to locate; mother and child in France.

Attempts made through legal channels to bring child to Switzerland in custody of father. Mother refuses access. Child's health and emotional state feared deteriorating.

Contempt of court cited against mother: Swiss courts have no jurisdiction in France. Matter taken to French courts.

Based on this physician's fears about the grave state of child's health, French courts issued temporary custody order. Mother cannot be located.

Authorities unable to enforce order. This physician, as child's father, unable to tolerate situation; on own initiative, travels to Paris, France. In compliance with orders from two courts, and on moral and medical grounds, child will be taken from mother.

Child returns to Switzerland, despite threats from mother. Emotional state of child intolerably aggravated by stress of home life (or lack thereof). Episodes of hyperventilation. Weight down to dangerous level. Pallor; agitation, anxiety. Treatment: oxygen for emergencies, nutrition, fresh air, exercise.

There were a few very recent notes about medication and vitamin therapy, and a progressive record of weight gain.

Heather finished the report and stared thoughtfully out of the window. There was little doubt about the agony concealed behind those terse notations. It was a story even more heartbreaking than the usual ones in these cases of marital breakdown. Few such stories had the poignancy of this one: a sick child left to the tender mercies of a woman like Geraldine . . . desperately fought for by her father who knew the consequences of neglect could be severe, if not fatal.

Why would Geraldine insist on taking the child? Heather knew her interest was not a maternal one;

she knew this with certainty as she had met Geraldine often enough to see very clearly her selfish nature. A chill passed through her at the thought of little Susie being dragged from resort to glamorous resort, living in a world of stale cigarette smoke and wound-down cocktail parties, able to rely on no one but the icy Geraldine for love.

Heather remembered Geraldine's words that day on the clinic doorstep: "I didn't know you had a neurotic kid." No wonder Susie was "neurotic"! No wonder she was shy with strangers, as Anton had said.

Heather realized that this file cast a whole new light on Anton Valdemar's relationship with his wife. And perhaps it revealed something about the hidden anger he seemed to carry within. . . .

There was a muted buzzing from the telephone. Startled, Heather eyed it uncertainly. Was she expected to answer it? After two or three rings she decided she had better.

"Is Dr. Valdemar there?" a woman asked in a peremptory tone. The voice was easily identifiable after a few seconds. It was Geraldine. . . .

"He's—not available at the moment. May I take a message?"

"This is his wife. Tell him I'll be up there this afternoon. And he'd better be ready to see me. Just tell him that."

"Certainly," said Heather very politely.

Without bothering to say goodbye, Geraldine hung up.

Slowly, Heather put the phone down. She was beginning to see what Anton Valdemar was up against in this woman. The telephone voice had been stripped of Geraldine's usual counterfeit charm. There was a steely quality to it, a hard-edged determination.

Anton stuck his head into the office. "Still going over the files? Was that anything important?" He nodded toward the telephone.

"Well, it was your wife. . . ."

He stepped into the room, his face clouded. "And what did she have to say?" A muscle twitched in his jaw, and his body had taken on the tenseness Heather had first seen in him.

"She said—she'd be up here this afternoon. And that you had better be 'ready'."

His scowl deepened, but he said nothing. Heather noticed that his fists, held rigidly at his sides, were tightly clenched.

"I'm sorry," Heather said hurriedly, "perhaps I should have called you."

But he dismissed her apology. "It's not important." Decisively, he strode across the office to the desk where Heather sat. "Now then. How's it going? Do you think you have some kind of general picture of the kids?"

"I've been through all the files—enough for now, anyway." Heather replied. "Now all I have to do is learn which child is which."

"They're all very individual—but you know that already. Do you want to come along now and engage in the minor warfare we call lunchtime around here?"

The noon meal was indeed quite a skirmish. Some of the children were very little, and spilled their milk with appalling regularity. They forgot what they were doing with their sandwiches, and dipped them into their soup. Heather enlisted some of the older children to regulate things a bit.

There were fourteen of them altogether, and when it was over Heather collapsed for a moment with Mrs. Rykman.

"I don't know how you ever did it!" she exclaimed.

The nurse, a plump and comfortable woman who seemed entirely unruffled by the antics of her charges, laughed. "You'll get used to it. The doctor isn't one of these rigid types who insists that nurses do all the dirty work. He pitches in, as you saw. And I'd rather see them throwing their food at each other like regular kids than moping around thin and pale. Means they're getting better."

"I suppose you're right," Heather said, mopping some tomato off her blouse. "What do we do now?"

"Well, as you probably know, the main problem with these children is the anxiety that comes with asthma attacks. They get scared they can't breathe, so they gulp air too quickly, causing the lungs to close up even more. Then the wheezing gets worse, and so on. It's a self-defeating spiral. We have to teach them to control the urge to hyperventilate— to breathe too deeply.

"Then we have supervised play therapy to help the children achieve a strong sense of personal identity. They learn to deal with their parents' anxiety. Last of all, before they go home, the parents usually come here to participate in some of the exercises. But that's only after the kids have built up considerable physical and mental health. Usually it takes several months."

"This is a wonderful clinic," Heather remarked. "Surely it's very expensive—I mean, it must have been expensive to build."

"Oh, yes. And there's little government funding for small projects like this one."

"Is it large enough? I mean, are all the facilities used, all the rooms?"

"Not yet. There's still space on the upper level.

But we can't expand till we can afford staff. Luckily, you volunteered, or we wouldn't even have this much help."

Mrs. Rykman got up reluctantly from her chair. "And right now," she added cheerfully, "I've got plenty to do. Want to come along? I'll show you the stuff for craft activities and such."

Heather spent the afternoon mixing paints and answering questions. She mopped up spills and rescued scissors from ill-coordinated small hands. Some of the children napped for a while, to her relief. When dinner time came, she was physically worn out.

Again, there was the chaos and chatter, the spills and refusals to eat. But at last the children were safely fed and bathed. By seven o'clock those who needed to go to bed had done so, and peace descended on the glass-walled clinic.

Heather flopped on a chair outside, stretching her legs before her. Around the horizon the frosty peaks of mountains caught flamingo-colored rays of sun. Shadows drew deep and long across the meadow grass.

She didn't hear Anton Valdemar approaching her. She jumped a little when he spoke.

"Still the eager volunteer?"

She looked up at him. His face was drawn and serious.

"Of course," she said. "I'm just a little pooped. We rich playgirls have quite a time adjusting to physical labor." She smiled wearily.

His eyes watched her thoughtfully. "I'm sorry about that. About saying you weren't the type. You're really very good with the children."

"So I'm hired?"

"You're hired. I wish I could pay you something—it doesn't seem right."

"Don't worry about that, please. I told you, it's the experience I need."

"All available funds have gone into the building," he said. "I'm hoping things will improve."

So Anton Valdemar did not have endless supplies of money. . . . It was easy to see why, she told herself, admiring the clinic once more. Already it struck Heather as ludicrous to suspect this man of being a criminal mastermind. He was obviously devoted to this project and the children's welfare.

Anton was staring thoughtfully across the meadow. She could see deep lines of worry around his eyes. Suddenly she remembered the phone call from Geraldine. She had been too busy all afternoon to notice whether the woman had come for her promised visit or not. She supposed that Geraldine had come, probably while Heather had been in the craft rooms with the older children.

"I guess your wife came by as planned," she said recklessly.

He looked down at her, the strain evident in his glance. "Oh, yes, she did that all right." He shrugged his wide shoulders. "She's my wife—in name only as they say." But he would not elaborate. "You had better be leaving if you want to get to town before dark," he said and turned to go.

Slowly, Heather got into her car, and backed out onto the road. Whatever Geraldine was up to, one thing was certain: her tentacles reached deeply into this man's life. She was making it a minor hell for him.

Chapter 9

When Heather arrived at her street, she found Malcolm's car parked by the corner. He waved at her to stop.

"I've been waiting for you," he said as he clambered in beside her. "I didn't want you to go home where I'd have to telephone you."

"Sorry I'm so late. What's the matter?"

"A number of things have come up. I'm due in Geneva in two hours to catch the late flight to Paris. But we've had a couple of breaks and I wanted to warn you."

"You have to go to Paris?"

"Yes. A number of operatives in other countries have come up with evidence that may tie in with what I've got. I'll be gone a day or two. It's very important that you know this and suspend your private-eye activities until I get back."

"Why? What have you found out?"

Malcolm took a deep breath. "Well, number one, it looks as if your friend Frederic's death may not have been entirely accidental after all."

Heather stared at him, her eyes wide with alarm. "Not—not an accident?"

He looked at her gravely. "Probably not. We have an idea there's an internal split in the ring of thieves. They may be warring over the diamonds— the Mogul Stars. Frederic was probably part of the faction that wanted to break away. Accidents like his can be engineered easily enough. The point is, though, that these people are desperate. They've broken a long tradition, a sort of thieves' code, not to murder." He took Heather firmly by the shoulders. "There's no telling what they might do to anyone who stumbled into their path."

Heather's lips trembled. She was temporarily speechless. Frederic . . . *murdered!*

"Now promise me—just lie low," Malcolm spoke urgently. "There's nothing to attract their attention to you, yet. But if you go making inquiries in Zurich . . . did you do anything about that, by the way?"

"No. . . . I didn't have a minute to myself today."

He gave a thin smile of relief. "How did it go at the clinic?"

Heather tried to think. "It was fine, really. I'm beginning to think we're wrong about Dr. Valdemar."

"I hope so. Otherwise, I wouldn't want you to go up there again."

"I *have* to go. They need me. You've no idea how overworked they are."

"Good. Then just go on with your work for a day or two. The case may break very soon with the evidence I've got to compare with the boys at headquarters. Then we'll see."

"I didn't see her," Heather said, "but Geraldine

came by the clinic this afternoon. Anton doesn't seem very fond of her. In fact, just the opposite. She may be using him in some way, though. He's extremely angry with her—a sort of rage or frustration boils in him. It may have to do with Susie, their child. They had a terrible battle over the custody. . . ."

Malcolm looked grimmer still. "That woman's in the thick of it, somehow. We haven't got any records on her. It's all very tenuous, like threads in a spider's web. A connection here and there, in Paris, Monte Carlo, London. She's 'very international,' as they say. But there's nothing to pin her down. No evidence, dammit. And she's not the mastermind. There's someone else behind it—someone who's more than clever."

"It's beginning to give me the creeps," shuddered Heather.

"Me, too. And I've seen a lot of them. Too bad we didn't begin watching this Geraldine sooner. Her name is Dumas, by the way."

"*Dumas*? But that's Celine's last name!"

"You noticed. A mother-daughter combination, perhaps."

"That does it. There *is* a connection with the house!" Heather's heart had begun to pound painfully. "But Geraldine has never contacted Celine—I mean, as far as I know. How could I know? I've been staying away from there as much as possible."

"Perhaps she wouldn't openly contact the woman. But it means you've got to be absolutely cool as a cucumber around Celine."

"An inscrutable mask, that's me. But what if Celine did overhear us that day in the bedroom? That means—"

"She may be very much on guard," Malcolm finished. "But you've got to manage to play dumb just a little longer. I don't really want her to know I've left town, either. If our cover is blown I don't want her to know how far we've got. If they panic and start making overt moves it might bring the person we're really looking for into the open—but it might also be the start of some very rough dealings."

Heather was silent. Things were moving fast—too fast. She could barely take it all in. Had it been Celine, after all, that night in the old house? And how was she using the house—Aunt Rachel's house—to further her criminal activities?

Frightened to death: the phrase came cruelly, vividly, into Heather's mind. Aunt Rachel had been frightened to death so that these criminals might carry on in peace whatever they were doing.

Her resolve was strengthened with this sudden insight. She was ready to do whatever was necessary to find the answers to the riddle.

She sat up very straight. "Okay. So what now?"

"I guess the best thing is for you to carry on working for Valdemar. You'll be away from Celine at least. And away from the house. I've looked at the old plans. They don't include the original building, but they do tell us a bit about the newer place. There's something funny about the way it was built, something not quite clear in the architect's drawings. The drawings may have even been falsified. I'm taking them to Paris to have tests made on the paper and the ink."

"Do you think there's a secret room, or something like that?"

"Sounds romantic, but I wouldn't discount the possibility. You see, those religious struggles a few centuries ago had lots of ramifications. Protestants hid from Catholics, Catholics from Protestants. There are stories of old hidey-holes for the priests, tunnels to hide church valuables. There was a lot of vandalism. And everybody was deadly serious: witness the burnings for heresy and witchcraft.

"And later on," continued Malcolm, "people used the old tunnels in these towns for other things—to hide arms and ammunition in wartime, or for outlaws on the run. I'm not talking about legends or fairy tales, Heather. These things are well documented. But I can't find anything specific about this town, about Sion itself."

"What if you do find out that the house plans from the archives are faked?" Heather asked.

"Then we'll begin looking more carefully at those foundations. Measure everything inside and out. Look for discrepancies. A hidden room or a tunnel, perhaps, leading to the cathedral . . . who knows? That might be the source of those noises in the night. Sound travels in strange ways. Acoustical effects could carry right up to your bedroom."

"It's all so fantastic," Heather sighed. "If people were underground, why wouldn't the sounds come from the floor? Why do they seem to come straight out of that old wardrobe?"

"It's odd, all right. You're certain you never heard them come from anywhere else?"

"No, neither did Aunt Rachel. She mentioned the wardrobe, too."

"Well, acoustical distortions are likely; and fairly common. When I get back we'll move that wardrobe, somehow. I'd like to take a look behind the thing."

"I'd like to investigate it tonight."

"You can't. It's too heavy. And you can't bring

anyone into the house to help because of Celine. She'd catch on for sure if she's hiding anything. No, you've got to wait." He looked at his watch. "And I've got to go. I'll be tearing up that highway to Geneva as it is."

"Malcolm?"

He looked at her, his brow creased with worry.

"*You* be careful, okay?"

He looped an arm around her awkwardly. "Heather, I—"

"Don't say anything, Malcolm."

"All right. I won't." He struggled out of the cramped little car. "Goodbye. I'll see you in a couple of days."

THREE DAYS PASSED, then four. Heather went about her duties at the clinic feeling distracted and worried. She would go home at night and sleep restlessly after a few wary words with Celine. If Celine had noticed that Malcolm wasn't coming around she didn't say so. The housekeeper went silently about her duties, seemingly as complacent as ever. Only her eyes, hooded and watchful, betrayed the slightest interest in Heather's comings and goings.

There were no noises.

In her distraction over the upside-down fantasy world of thieves and killers and international intrigue, Heather found herself turning to the children more and more.

They saw things simply in terms of colors and sounds and beauty. They chattered endlessly, or listened with rapt fascination to the stories Heather read aloud. Some of them, thin and fragile, seemed to bloom, to become more robust even as she watched them play.

She was becoming increasingly interested, too, in the children's therapy sessions with Anton and Mrs. Rykman. These were painful to watch sometimes, but Heather was learning to handle her feelings. She remembered a great deal of the theory she had learned at college. It was demanding but rewarding work, and at times Heather even found peace.

It was still difficult to absorb the reality behind Frederic's masquerade, and the basic falsehoods that had fooled her completely. But at least now the pain and the feelings of guilt were fading rapidly.

Heather found herself especially drawn to Susie, Anton's child. Susie had a specialness about her, an air of grave defensive serenity. She played quietly for hours with modeling clay, or painted wildly colorful pictures that displayed the ghosts and ambivalences of her inner world. There were tall stick figures, featuring pipe and hat, under a radiant pie-in-the-sky sun. When asked, she would say solemnly that this was her daddy. There were flowers and great soaring birds beside him and in the blue-washed sky.

And there were pictures of the lady, the one Susie wouldn't name. The lady, painted with splashes of purple and brown, occupied almost all of Susie's paper. She had yellow hair, and her eyes were studiously outlined with long, spikey lashes.

The lady, Heather knew, was Susie's mother.

Susie was slowly working out her feelings about Geraldine. Anton looked at these pictures with care. He never commented, but Heather knew he was concerned with the child's progress, and her reaction to being separated from her mother. For she *was* separated, very conscientiously, from Geraldine. Heather found this out when the woman came again to call on Anton.

It was during an afternoon play session that Heather was supervising in the meadow. She had just looked up and registered the fact that a car was approaching along the road.

The clinic door swung open and Mrs. Rykman ran down the steps. She waved urgently at Heather and signaled that she should bring Susie in. Without hesitation Heather scooped the child up, still clutching at her wooden animals from the Noah's ark she had been playing with. She ran with her to Mrs. Rykman and delivered her to the woman's arms.

In an instant the two had disappeared inside the building. Heather turned to study the car. It was the large powerful model Geraldine had driven that first day, but Geraldine wasn't alone. She was accompanied by a man who wore numerous gold neck chains. Heather recognized him almost immediately; he had been with her that day at the inn when Heather first discovered that Geraldine was visiting Sion.

Geraldine braked the car to a reckless halt, and jumped out. She strode toward Heather, her every step a study in seething anger. "You again!" she said in a low grating voice. Her eyes bored into Heather's. "What are you doing here? And what makes you think you can interfere with *my* child? He's got her here against my will. She's *my* daughter I tell you!"

Before Heather could respond, Geraldine whirled impatiently and stomped up the stairs. The clinic door slammed.

Heather glanced at the man in the car, who smiled appraisingly at her. Cheeks burning, she turned away and hurried back across the meadow to the children.

It was some time before Anton Valdemar's wife reappeared. Heather watched warily as she came out of the clinic.

Geraldine stood on the stairs, and across the distance separating them Heather thought she felt waves of malevolence. The woman stared for a few deliberate moments, then walked briskly to her car. As she drove away Mrs. Rykman appeared at the door, watching the car disappear.

The incident was not mentioned until after the children's supper that evening. The nurse sat sipping coffee with Heather on the terrace. She made a few inconsequential remarks about the day's work, but Heather could see that she was leading up to something.

At last she seemed to make a decision to speak her mind. "Heather," she began. "There's something I want to talk to you about, if you're going to be one of us here at the clinic."

"Yes? What is it?"

"It's about Dr. Valdemar . . . and Susie. I'm a little hesitant to talk about it because I know he wouldn't, but—well, it's become important, something of a crisis. You saw what happened this afternoon with that woman in the car. We had to take Susie in. . . ."

Heather nodded encouragingly.

"Well, you must have wondered why that was. You'll wonder even more when I tell you that woman is Susie's mother."

"Really?" Heather feigned a look of mild surprise.

"She's Susie's mother, all right," Mrs. Rykman continued, "but I can assure you that she has no right to be—no right to the child, that is. The poor doctor," she sighed.

"Do you mean there's some sort of dispute over the child?" Heather prompted.

"Yes. They've been separated ever since Susie was two. It was a terrible marriage. I happen to know because I've worked with Dr. Valdemar for a good many years. It was one of those—mistakes. A young man struggling to get himself established in practice and this stunning creature comes along, Geraldine Dumas. Said she was from Paris. I don't know about that. I shouldn't say this but she told him she was going to have his baby so they got married.

"She made him miserable from the first. But he had his work, and his daughter, Susie. Then Geraldine ran off, back to her old haunts, I guess. She took Susie with her. She always told me she was bored stiff in Sion. But then why would she marry a man like Anton, someone who likes the country and simple things, real things?" The nurse looked at Heather in mystification and dismay.

Heather gave a gentle shrug of understanding.

"Anyway," Mrs. Rykman continued, "she took Susie out of spite, I say. The doctor was frantic. He wanted the child back, more for her own sake than his. The poor mite was sick even then. But he had nursed her along devotedly. Her mother had always paid her scant attention.

"He knew—he *knew* Susie would suffer terribly, sharing the kind of life that Geraldine Dumas was interested in.

"He wrote and phoned and sent telegrams to his wife. He pleaded with her. She could have whatever she wanted, except the child. You see, he always had a little money, from his family, and he was trying to raise more, because this clinic had always been a dream of his. He went to Paris, to Rome, to the south of France—wherever he thought he might find her.

"But she was so clever. She always eluded him, always got away from him. And she always dragged Susie with her." The woman's face was clouded with anger as she told Anton's story.

Heather could feel a knot of tension growing within her. This was the same story, told in human terms, as she had read in Anton's file on Susie. It was the real tragedy behind those terse, professional notations.

"Finally," said Mrs. Rykman, "he went to the courts. It's routine for a divorce court to award custody of a child to the mother, unless she can be proved wildly unfit, and he didn't want to risk losing Susie forever. But Geraldine was playing it very dirty. He had to testify against his wife, for the child's sake.

"There were a lot of legal technicalities. He couldn't get a divorce in absentia, but he tried to persuade them on medical grounds to order Geraldine to bring Susie back to Switzerland for a hearing. Finally, after a lot of hemming and hawing, they did. They issued court orders here and in France. But even that did no good. Geraldine just didn't give a damn." The nurse paused for a long sip of her coffee, then went on.

"I can tell you, Anton Valdemar became a changed man. He was stormy, angry. He began building this place to take care of children like Susie—and one day, he hoped, Susie herself. But no one could talk to him anymore. He had only one thing on his mind, and he worked day and night for it. I grieved for him; he's so strong, so good, but this other business nearly destroyed him emotionally.

"Then, not two months ago, his chance came. He scrounged up enough to pay someone to locate Geraldine. She never stayed in one place long enough for the court officers to be able to even serve a writ.

"But one day his detective informed Anton that his wife was in France. They managed to locate Susie. She was parked with an appalling woman while Geraldine was out for the evening. And he stole her—stole his own child away. He brought her back here."

"Not that he was safe. International law frowns on kidnapping no matter who does it."

Heather nodded silently, her emotions churning.

The nurse's eyes shone with tears. "Geraldine has been coming up here, looking for Susie. She says she's going to have him prosecuted. He has no safe position legally, and she knows it. She screams at him, threatens him. I don't know how long it's going to go on. I can hardly take the worry my-self . . . I can imagine how he's feeling." The nurse's hands were trembling as she wiped away the tears that had started to overflow.

Impulsively, Heather reached out to her, and put a firm hand on her arm. "It's all right, Mrs. Ryk-man, we'll all fight her. . . ."

The nurse seemed to gather strength from the contact. She took a deep breath. "He won't let her have Susie, and I won't either!" She looked at Heather with pleading eyes. "Don't let him know I've told you all this. He's such—such a private sort of man. But now you can help, can't you?

You're a strong, competent girl. And he trusts you, I can see that. He's ignored women for a long time, but . . . but you're different."

Heather blushed deeply. "Oh, I don't . . . ."

"I know he likes you," the nurse said firmly. "But you must help. You see the big worry now is that she'll try to get Susie any way she can. Threats about the law are one thing, but he does have that court order for a custody hearing, and he has filed for divorce. The courts might listen to him."

"He's a doctor, after all, a man whose word they *should* take. . . . I think she knows that. And she would go very far to hurt him. She doesn't love that child; it's all for spite. I'm sure she's planning to steal the child back."

Heather stared at Mrs. Rykman in the evening silence. "Do you think so?" she asked, her voice barely above a whisper. She shared every ounce of the nurse's tension and fear.

"Yes—and the doctor thinks so, too. He says Geraldine is never to come in contact with Susie, never to see her. You see she upsets the child terribly. Even talking about her mother can bring on an attack. Susie has been emotionally damaged by those three years of being dragged around in her mother's mindless pursuit of pleasure. She wasn't even fed properly."

"But, surely Geraldine has lots of money . . . that car—"

"Yes," said the nurse, now in full possession of herself again. "And where do you suppose she gets it? One of these sugar daddies they talk about?" Mrs. Rykman pursed her mouth.

I know where she gets it, thought Heather. But

she wasn't free to discuss this with anyone. Malcolm's investigation must not be jeopardized; she had been warned of the consequences. . . .

"Mrs. Rykman, you have all my support, believe me. And I won't say anything to Dr. Valdemar. You were right to tell me, and there's nothing I won't do to help." Heather paused, thinking quickly. "You know the first thing I ought to do is start staying at the clinic overnight. That way Geraldine will have three bodies to fight if she tries anything after dark." *And no more fencing with Celine*, she thought with relief.

"Good idea," said Mrs. Rykman, all competence again. "Come on. There's a room upstairs you can have." She picked up her coffee cup and rose from her chair, saying, "But what will we tell the doctor? I mean, I'm not really supposed to have told you all this about him. . . ."

"We can say that I'm tired of commuting. I'm sure he won't mind." Heather gave the nurse a reassuring pat, and together they went into the clinic. By now, dusk had fallen and all the lights were on. Trying to hide a child in this glass house at night could be difficult, Heather realized.

If only Malcolm would call . . . perhaps he would know what they should do. Where on earth could he be? He had said he would only be gone a couple of days, but tomorrow would make it five. Had he come back today, she wondered. She would have to telephone Celine to say she wouldn't be returning home. Was there some way she could ask if Malcolm had called without arousing her suspicions? She could adopt her "young girl in love" pose, but Celine wasn't supposed to have noticed that Malcolm was out of town. No, that wouldn't do. She would have to wait for him to telephone her. He knew she would be here at the clinic most of the time.

As expected, Celine was noncommittal when Heather informed her that she would be out for the night. Her voice over the telephone wire was even drier than usual. Cold, calculating, and—even at this distance—insinuating. Heather was glad to hang up.

She turned from the telephone to find Anton watching her, his tall body blocking the doorway. She was slightly disconcerted at the way his eyes, so gray and distant, seemed to read her every thought. "I—I thought I'd stay the night," she said nervously.

"So Mrs. Rykman tells me. Is it really all that much trouble to drive down to Sion? You've done it for several days without complaint." He was watching her closely, she realized.

"Well, it's a nuisance, and I'm rather tired. Besides, there are things to do around here even after the day is supposed to be over."

"Don't you think that's a bit beyond the call of duty? You're a volunteer. We don't expect this much of you."

"Oh, I know you don't *expect* it but . . . ." Heather was confused. There was something in his eyes, something that glinted dangerously. . . .

"I think you really should go home," he said quietly. It was an order not a suggestion.

What could be bothering him? *Perhaps*, Heather thought with sudden clarity, *he's suspicious of me. I'm a relative stranger, working here on my own initiative. Maybe he thinks I've got something to do with Geraldine—he's afraid of kidnapping—it*

*would be easy enough for him to think that I'm
part of a plot!*

But how could she reassure him without giving
away Mrs. Rykman's lack of 'discretion'?

There was nothing reasonable she could say, so
she resorted to simple stubbornness. "I'll have to
stay tonight, doctor. Even if it displeases you. It's
already dark and the lights on my car aren't
reliable."

"Is that so?" he asked softly, and Heather flushed
with embarrassment at the transparency of her
ploy. He wasn't fooled, and the harsh glint in his
eyes seemed to sharpen. Heather wanted only to
escape from the relentless, probing gaze.

"Yes, I'm afraid it is," she faltered. "Now if
you'll excuse me, I'll . . . ."

But he didn't stir. He continued to watch her, a
towering implacable presence in the doorway,
blocking her confused retreat. He tilted his head
back for a moment, his features becoming deeply
etched by shadows. It made him look angry,
almost fearsome. Heather forgot the pain she knew
lay behind those lines, forgot for a moment his
gentleness with the children. Her heart began to
race, and she trembled a little. She was reminded
of the mountains, of their stony, unreadable faces,
and their brooding presence out there in the
darkness. . . .

She stepped forward, trying to avoid his eyes.
"I'd better go now," she said in a small voice.

"No," he said moving toward her. Heather was
transfixed; she couldn't seem to will herself to
move or to speak.

"No," he repeated, and caught her to him. His

mouth found hers with a burning, bruising pressure.

Heather felt suspended, as if she were floating. The warmth of his body enveloped her and for a timeless moment the kiss softened, deepened. . . .

Without warning he released her. His eyes were filled with shadows as they searched her own. Heather could hear her own heartbeat, a drowning, thunderous roar in her ears. Her fingers, cool and alien, seemed to automatically raise themselves to her lips.

"Who are you? Where did you come from?" The words came raggedly, as if torn from his very being. Then abruptly, he turned and was gone from the room.

Heather stood in the silence, numbed by the intense feelings that washed over her. Slowly, her lips formed a single, whispered word.

"*Anton.*"

At last, her surroundings seemed to come into focus. Mechanically she walked from the room along the hall to the stairs. With slow-motion lightness, she climbed to the second floor, and found the room Mrs. Rykman had prepared for her. And, totally detached from what she was doing, she undressed and went to bed. All the while one word echoed insistently through her consciousness, obliterating all else.

Anton.

Chapter 10

Mrs. Rykman's fears for Susie were not exaggerated. Geraldine made her move the very next afternoon.

But the day had begun quietly enough. Anton had gone to town early. Heather awakened feeling disoriented in her strange room, her mind filled with thoughts of him. But when she went down to breakfast he had already left. She tried hard to hide her disappointment when Mrs. Rykman, bustling around the table with a box of cereal, told her the doctor wouldn't be back till later.

She held the memory of their encounter last night safely within her like some bright new coin. Occasionally, her mind examined it, then tucked it away. She was filled with elation.

This was new to her, the quiet certitude of it. Anton was troubled now, but later when he knew, when all the answers came out, and he realized he could trust her . . . .

She tried to concentrate on the children.

"He said he wouldn't be long," Mrs. Rykman

told her distractedly, tending the wants of a despondent youngster who refused, against all argument, to believe that orange juice was indeed what he needed this morning. "I've asked the girl from the village to stay awhile after lunch to help," she added. "We need to be as watchful as we can even in broad daylight." Her tone was light, so as not to alarm the children.

"Don't worry," smiled Heather. "Nobody will get past me. Will they, Susie?"

The little girl gave her an owlish look. "Where's daddy?" she asked.

"Mrs. Rykman just said. He went to town, but he won't be long. How about we all wash our hands and faces then go out to the meadow for our walk?"

Dubiously, Susie agreed.

The morning was spent in happy absorption. Never had Heather's mind been so clear, her thoughts so gentle as she watched the youngsters and helped them to find flowers, insects, birds' nests. Lunchtime, too, went by in a sweet sort of haze.

I never felt this way about Frederic, Heather said to herself with wonder. How could she have thought she loved Frederic at all? And how could she have misread those small signs—the little interior flutterings that told her before she knew it that she was attracted to Anton?

Well, it was all right now. Somehow everything would work out. When Malcolm came back the riddles would be solved. He had said they were very near to making a break in the case. And if he had any evidence against Geraldine . . . .

After lunch, the youngest went for their naps as

usual. Therapy sessions were temporarily canceled until Anton's return. Heather busied herself with setting up new activities for the older children. Susie was assigned to her paint box and miniature easel, which she attacked with solemn industry.

At last everything was arranged, every child engaged in something constructive. Heather decided to sit for a moment out in the sun.

She was lost in drowsy daydreams, a golden blend of the sun's warmth and her own thoughts. She failed to notice, at first, the hum of the car's motor. When she looked up, she was startled to see Geraldine's unmistakable big sedan only a few hundred feet down the road.

In a flash, Heather jumped out of the chair and flew up the steps almost before she had time to think. Running down the hallway she called for Mrs. Rykman and Helena, the girl from the village.

"Hurry," she urged. "Helena, you take Susie out the back way. They won't see you. Mrs. Rykman, come with me." Anxiously she watched as the village girl scooped Susie up and ran for the back door. It slammed, and through the glass, Heather saw her cover the distance to a dense clump of trees with gratifying speed.

Now stay there, she willed them silently. *Don't move, don't breathe.*

"Come on," she said urgently to Mrs. Rykman. "We're going to defend the front gate."

When they returned to the front hall, Geraldine had angrily shut the door behind her.

Imperiously, she glared at Heather and the nurse.

Then a slow knowing smile formed on her lips. "All right. You can scurry around as much as you like. But I know he isn't here. His car is gone. Now is as good a time as any for me to take my little darling home, don't you think?"

"She—she's not here. She went to town with Anton," Heather said, drawing herself up.

"With *Anton*?" Geraldine's voice was heavy with sarcasm as she gave Heather a withering look. "Well, isn't that nice? However, I don't believe you." She began to stalk down the hall, looking into rooms.

"You can't just walk in here and do this—" Mrs. Rykman cried, her jaw set aggressively.

Geraldine whirled. "And who's going to stop me? You, perhaps?"

"Yes, me," replied Mrs. Rykman, moving toward her.

"Oh, I wouldn't. Max, who is just outside, might have something to say about that."

As if on cue, the tanned man, his multitude of gold chains glinting, stepped in out of the sun.

"No kids outside," he said to Geraldine.

"Keep an eye on these two," Geraldine instructed shortly. "I'm going to check this place out."

Seething, Heather held her tongue. Let Geraldine poke around all she liked *inside*. Thank God Susie was safely hidden outside in those sheltering trees. Obviously Max hadn't thought to look there.

Waiting tensely, Heather hardly dared to breathe. Mrs. Rykman, agitated and angry, wrung her hands. The long moments dragged by as the clicking of Geraldine's heels echoed from room to room. The children, playing in the various work spaces, seemed to sense something was wrong. Their usual chatter was hushed. The only sound in fact was Max's low, insolent whistling, as he stood guarding them. At last Geraldine came clattering down the stairs having inspected every room in the place. She strode up to Heather and thrust her finger into her face.

"You did this. I don't know how, but you did. You won't get away with it!"

"Come on," Max said impatiently. "Today's just not your day, honey."

"I'll be back. You can tell *Anton* that." She glared at Heather once more, then stormed out.

Heather and the nurse watched in agonized suspense as they got into their car and drove away. They didn't cease their vigil until the car was well out of sight.

"Gone," Heather breathed. "Thank God!"

Together they rushed to the back door. Running across the grass, Heather called out eagerly. "Helena, it's all right. Susie, come out now!"

There was no stirring but wind in the little grove of trees.

Puzzled, Heather ran faster. "Helena! Susie!" The two women were both calling now. They reached the trees and plunged into their shelter. There was no answer to their cries. Frantically, Heather pushed branches aside, ignoring the scratches to her arms and face. Mrs. Rykman's sharp cries had faded to a low moan of terror.

They almost stepped on Helena before they saw her. She lay crumpled on the ground. Stunned, Heather knelt down and looked closely at her face. The girl's eyelids fluttered, and she groaned.

"Helena . . . Helena, please! What happened?"

Painfully, the girl opened her eyes. "Don't know," she managed to say. "They hit me . . . over the head. Susie—they took her!"

Heather's stomach gave a jolting wrench. A

black mist threatened to descend on her. She blinked and struggled hard to steady herself.

"Who?" she cried urgently. "Did you see them? Who was it Helena?"

Helena fought visibly for consciousness.

"*Please*, Helena. Did you see them?"

"Two men," gasped the girl. "I heard them. They came from behind. From the mountain."

From the mountain? So that was it! Geraldine, like some cunning general, had planned a two-pronged attack. The approach from the road—the one Heather had expected—was only a diversion. The real assault was from the rear, from the mountain side of the little meadow.

Heather's heart was leaden. Anton would be returning soon to discover his daughter had been kidnapped. . . . She was seared with helpless anguish.

Helena was sitting up now, supported by Mrs. Rykman. The girl was sobbing. "I'm sorry, I'm sorry." The nurse looked at Heather with eyes that were pools of despair.

"It wasn't your fault, Helena," Heather soothed. "I was the one who thought up this stupid plan. . . . Here, let Mrs. Rykman help you back to the clinic. I'm going after those men."

Mrs. Rykman's eyes widened still further. "But you can't—they're dangerous! Look what they did to her. . . ."

"I don't have any choice. Obviously they're on foot. And likely they're headed for the forest path down to Ferpècle. That's the only way they can go. I'm used to hiking over rocky trails, and maybe they're not. They've got a child to carry, too."

Ferpècle . . . yes, they had to be there. Geraldine

would be waiting in her car, ready to pick up her hired thugs.

"Get Helena into the house, then get back to the children," she said to Mrs. Rykman, who looked terrified. "Don't go falling apart on me now."

And Heather began to run as she had never done before in her life. She bounded up the rocky path behind the little grove. They had only a few minutes' start on her. If she could only cover this rough ground quickly enough . . . .

The path wound upward and then began to make its way sharply to the left. It would lead eventually to the place where she and Malcolm had picnicked just a few days ago when they had first seen Anton's clinic from afar.

Heather scrambled over the rocks, falling and scraping her hands repeatedly. Her breath was already coming in ragged gasps. She would never make it, never catch up to them!

She glanced down into the little valley. The clinic was clearly visible here from above, down a dizzy drop of a hundred feet. With sudden clarity, Heather realized that they must have been watching from this point, waiting for their chance—for who knew how many days?

She tripped again, violently, and fell against a jutting shoulder of rock. The pain tore through her, but she gritted her teeth and plunged on. No one was anywhere in sight. She heard only the sound of her own pounding footsteps and labored breathing.

But what was that?

Heather stood stock-still, listening. She had heard a voice. Yes, there it was again. She tried to locate it; it had come from dead ahead. There was a rocky abutment, a blind curve in the path. The voice had been indistinct, buffeted by the currents of the wind. But she heard it again, and she moved toward it with shaky caution.

She braced herself with both hands against the solid stone. Then with infinite care she moved one step at a time around the blind curve in the path. There was no turning back, even if they were waiting on the other side for her—waiting to smash something down on her head. . . . Trembling, she forced herself to think only of Susie. And she kept moving.

The sound came again. Undistorted, she recognized it as a man's voice: a voice shot through with agony! Rapidly, she pulled herself around the last few feet of the curved abutment.

Malcolm!

He lay beside the path, propped grotesquely against a ledge. He was breathing with great, tearing gasps, and trying desperately to sit himself upright. A moan of pain, the sound Heather had been hearing, escaped him each time he moved.

"Malcolm! What—what on earth?" She knelt beside him trying to support him. She saw the blood then. A terrifying amount of it soaking the front of his shirt. Panting, he lifted his head.

"Heather . . ." he breathed.

"Shh, it's me. You're bleeding—you'll bleed to death." Thinking quickly, remembering thankfully some long-ago first-aid course, she pulled off the lightweight jacket she was wearing and rolled it into a ball. She stuffed it firmly against the shoulder, which she could see now was the source of the bleeding.

Malcolm sucked in a huge swallow of air. "They shot me," he gasped, managing a lopsided parody of a grin. "I told you they were going to play rough. . . ."

"They've taken Susie," Heather said urgently. "Anton's little girl."

"I know . . . about the little girl. Know why they took her, too."

"I've got to catch them, Malcolm. I've got to go after them."

"You can't. It—it's too late. They're gone by now . . . in the car."

"Gone? They haven't had enough time."

"They have. There's a short path. I've been . . . watching them . . . watching *you* down there . . . for two days. Thought I could stop them, though. Didn't think they'd get this far."

He looked directly at her, and his eyes seemed to focus properly for the first time since she had found him. "Heather! It's all right. I know where they've gone."

"You do?"

"Yes. Things clicked together in Paris. Found out nearly all I need to know about Geraldine . . . about the house. But help me up. We've got to get down off this path . . . to the clinic. I've got a bullet in me. Come on, *push*." He shuddered with the pain, but they struggled until he was upright. Woozily, he staggered along while Heather supported him and held the jacket as well as she could against the wound. After an eternity of slow painful progress they reached the clinic.

Anton had not returned, and Mrs. Rykman, when she had recovered from this latest shock,

shook her head gravely as she examined Malcolm's
wound. Together, she and Heather laid him out on
a bed. He was weak and barely lucid now.

"The little girl," he said, clutching Heather's
hand, while the nurse pressed new dressings on the
bullet wound. "To get the little girl you have to go
back to town. I know where they are, these people,
where they will hide her. Will hide her for
sure . . . ." He closed his eyes.

"He's lost too much blood," said Mrs. Rykman
tersely. "The ambulance should be here soon. I'd
better see if it's not too late to tell them to bring
extra O-type blood with them," said the nurse as
she hurried out of the room.

"Heather . . . ." Malcolm's eyes were open again.
"The old wardrobe . . . move it. Get it moved
right away. It leads down—leads to where they
will take her. Go that way, not through the
church. You can surprise them, catch them when
they think . . . think they're safe." His voice
wandered, and it seemed he was about to lose
consciousness. Clutching her hand he fought back.
"And don't go alone. . . ." He drifted away,
lapsing into incoherence."

Mrs. Rykman was back. "I've been trying to find
Dr. Valdemar, but he's not at the hospital. I don't
know what to do. . . ."

"What you had better do is keep an eye on this
man. Don't leave him. If Anton returns tell him
I've gone after Susie, that I know where she is. Tell
him the old house. My Aunt Rachel's house."

She stood up. Just as she turned to go Malcolm
again tried to speak. "Go to the house. The
wardrobe . . . behind it. The boat . . . don't
forget. . . ." His voice had faded so they could
hardly hear him.

"Don't talk anymore," the nurse ordered. "Go on, Heather. He's delirious. If you know where the child is, *go*."

HEATHER TOOK EVERY TURN on the road to Sion with breakneck speed. She pressed her foot to the floor on the straight stretches. Her brain was racing far ahead as she impatiently clocked the miles. The wardrobe? She had to move it. Was this Malcolm's secret passage, then? It seemed totally weird. He was delirious, after all. Might he not have mixed everything up? Perhaps he was hopelessly confused in his own subconscious?

But he had seemed so sure of it, sure they would take her there, to this medieval hiding place somewhere under the house. It was her only chance she decided. The one chance to catch these people off guard.

Heather's knuckles were white as she clutched the steering wheel. The motor raced as she pulled into town, down Haute Street toward her house.

She would need help. But who could help?

She passed a familiar cul-de-sac and impulsively slammed on the brakes. Oscar! His shop was only a few feet along this street. He would help. She got out of the car, raced along the cobblestones, and threw herself against the door of the little shop.

He looked up in surprise as she stumbled in. "Oscar, you've got to come, come quickly," she gasped. "Please hurry. They've kidnapped her, Dr. Valdemar's little girl."

"What? Slow down. Who has kidnapped the little girl?"

"Some criminals. I can't explain now. I've got to get to my house, move Aunt Rachel's old wardrobe—oh, Oscar, please, just *come!*"

"All right, I'm coming." He clapped his battered old hat onto his head. "Jacques," he called into the room behind, "come take care of things. . . ."

"You come, too," Heather ordered the man who emerged from the back room. "We need somebody strong!"

The man looked at Oscar in questioning amazement, but Oscar made a quick, impatient movement. "Come along. I don't know what it is, but we'll do as she says. Let's go."

They crowded into Heather's little car and careened recklessly through the streets to Rachel Savorin's house. Heather hardly bothered to switch off the ignition. She stumbled blindly up the front steps, her heart pounding painfully. The key wouldn't turn properly for a few agonizing seconds, but at last she got the door open.

Celine! She had forgotten about her. Heather expected the woman to be in the hall, somehow blocking her way. But Celine didn't matter any more. She could be dealt with later. . . .

The house echoed to their pounding footsteps, yet Celine did not appear.

The men galloped along close behind her as Heather took the stairs two at a time. She tore along the hall and into the bedroom with them at her heels.

"Here! Here it is! Malcolm says to move this aside and we'll find it."

"Find what?" Oscar asked, frowning at the great bulk of the old armoire.

Heather's urgency almost choked her words off. "I don't know, I—Malcolm just told me to move it."

Oscar, puffing a little from his run, cocked an

eyebrow at her. Then he shrugged. "All right. Move it we will. Jacques, you get that end—"

"Here, I'll help." Heather thrust a shoulder against one end. Oscar and Jacques cursed and muttered. But at last the stubborn thing began to move. Inch by inch the gap between its back and the wall widened.

Anxiously, Heather peered into the dark space behind. She could see nothing, only faded wallpaper. The wardrobe was shoved far enough aside for her to slip into the space behind it.

The wall was blank! A sort of crazy despair flooded through her. Nothing! Malcolm had been delirious after all. She had come storming all the way here for no reason at all. Angrily, Heather pounded the dusty wall.

Bits of wallpaper, dry as bone, crumbled away under her fists.

She flattened her palms, filled with a new excitement. A straight, thin crack had appeared. She felt along it, her fingers dancing, trembling. Yes, the paper cracked away for a foot or two in this direction . . . her hands flew to the other side. Yes! there it was. As she pressed, the rough rectangular outline of a door appeared.

"What's going on?" Oscar asked from behind her. "What have you found?"

"It's a door! Malcolm was right! There's something here. I don't know what it leads to. . . . See?" She stood aside so Oscar could have a look.

He peered at the wall for a moment, giving it a couple of experimental taps. "Well, I'll be darned. Jacques, look at this."

The other man took a turn standing in the space they had opened behind the old armoire.

Heather was in an agony of impatience. "Can't we try to open it?"

Oscar was all business. "Yes. Yes, we'll do that. But we need a thing or two . . . a light, a crowbar or a hammer. . . ."

Heather was off downstairs before he could finish. She found the things they needed and ran back up to the room. They were working away at the crack with pocket knives. When Heather gave them the hammer and screwdrivers they set to work in earnest.

Soon the entire door was revealed, and Oscar was able to wedge one of the screwdrivers in to loosen it.

"Wait," he mumbled. "I see." Measuring with his eye he began to tear away paper from one of the inner panels. See? Here's where the knob and latch was. It's an old one, not very sophisticated. The latch is still intact inside that hole. Just needs a lever. . . ." Grimacing, he poked the screwdriver into the hole and turned it. There was a grating sound, then a metallic click.

Oscar gave the door a hard shove. With a clatter of falling plaster and wood fragments it began to open. Heather pressed both hands to her mouth. What would they find beyond?

Susie. This was the way to Susie!

Anxiously she handed Oscar the flashlight. He shone it into the darkness. The first thing they saw was a masonry wall. It was a door to nowhere! Again, Heather's heart plummeted.

But then Oscar shone the light downward. Heather could make out the first few steps of a rough staircase.

Oscar turned to her questioningly. "Now what? Do we go down into that hole?"

"We have to. Let me go first." Without permitting him to protest she seized the light and pushed past them through the opening. "Coming?"

"Well, why not?" Oscar mumbled.

"But be quiet. I don't know what we'll find."

Stumbling in the darkness behind her, the men followed. The staircase wound straight down for two floors, Heather judged. And then it stopped.

But it couldn't be! She couldn't be stopped now. "This *can't* be all there is," she whispered angrily.

"Now *I'm* curious," muttered Oscar. "Give me that light and come back up here so I can get down."

Heather obeyed him. He shone the flashlight over all the corners of the dead-end stairwell. Then he stooped and very carefully examined the floor. "These boards are recent enough. I can tell by the nails. Let's lift one and see. Jacques, go get the hammer." The other man did as he was told.

"No hope of being quiet, I'm afraid," Oscar said, giving one of the boards a mighty yank. It squeaked loudly, and Heather grimaced. But she was anxious to see what lay under the floor. The passage had to continue; it *had* to lead somewhere.

Heather was not disappointed. The lifted boards revealed a large empty space below.

"Here, Jacques. Get down there, and see what you can see."

They shifted positions, and Jacques slipped through the hole, gripping the edge with his hands. Oscar held the light down for him.

"Okay. I'm going to drop now," Jacques said.

The hands disappeared, and she heard the light smack of his shoes on a floor. It was a flat sound, as if the floor were stone.

"Aha!" said Oscar. "A mysterious subterranean room. Is this what you were looking for?"

"I don't know. It must be. Let me go next," she said quickly.

"Just let yourself down by your arms," Oscar instructed. "That's right. Now you can let go. It's not a far drop, is it Jacques?"

"No," the man answered, his voice echoing hollowly.

Heather braced herself and let go. She landed lightly enough with the same dull smack Jacques had made.

Oscar was still shining the light down. "I think I'll come, too. Catch this."

Jacques nimbly caught the flashlight, and Oscar came down with a somewhat heavier thud. He stood up and brushed off the dust. "This is a most interesting exploration," he said. "Don't you think, Jacques?"

"Amazing," the other man agreed.

"But this doesn't lead us anywhere," Heather cried angrily. "I've got to find Susie—"

"Shh!" said Oscar, holding a finger to his lips. "Did you hear something?"

Breathlessly, Heather listened. Yes, she could hear something, something muffled, tentative, far off, and yet very near. . . . Those noises!

She stood frozen in the darkness of the room, then turned to face the sounds.

"Over there," whispered Oscar, shining the flashlight straight at the wall ten feet away. In it there was a deeper blackness similar to the entrance to a tunnel.

Oscar switched off the flashlight.

The noises approached, closer and closer. Gradually, Heather began to distinguish footsteps and voices. They were coming! Was it Geraldine with Susie? With those thugs of hers and the man with the gold chains?

Suddenly Heather grew cold with a new fear. She was standing here with an old man, and with Jacques—they had nowhere to hide, nothing to protect themselves with.

The voices grew nearer. They would be here soon. She could see their light.

"Oscar," she whispered, "we've got to hide. They've got guns. . . ."

He touched her arm, signaling silence. But he made no move.

The lights swelled, filling the passageway. It was too late. Bizarre shadows danced on the rough walls at the mouth of the tunnel.

Then the lights flooded blindingly into the room. Heather squinted. For a moment she could make out nothing.

Then she saw Susie. She was a limp bundle, carried by a short man. The child's head lolled, but Heather couldn't be sure whether it was in sleep or unconsciousness. Angrily, her eyes sought Geraldine's presence.

Geraldine moved forward, staring in surprise. But her gaze was fixed on Oscar. . . .

"Papa!" she cried. "What on earth are you doing here?"

"Well you may wonder, daughter dear, since you

have so recklessly brought this young lady down on our heads."

Heather turned to stare at Oscar. She couldn't believe her ears. *Papa*? Geraldine had called Oscar papa!

Oscar smiled at Heather, his features grotesquely heightened in the uncertain light.

"I'm sorry to have to tell you this, but this wicked young woman is my daughter. And after all I have tried to teach her about discretion in this business she has brought alarms on us from everywhere."

He turned to face Geraldine again, and the mask of politeness evaporated. "You stupid creature! What are you doing here with that child?" he roared. "Don't you realize they'll come after her?"

Geraldine quailed, but stood her ground. "It was the only safe place. I had to do it. She wouldn't let go of the damned toy."

"Well, did you get *that*, at least?" Oscar's voice filled the low-ceilinged room. Geraldine's group huddled together opposite him, their faces contorted by the bobbing flashlights. Heather could see that they were all afraid of him . . . of Oscar!

Geraldine hadn't spoken, but she held an object out toward him. With a savage gesture he tore it from her hands.

Heather recognized it immediately. The Noah's ark! Susie's favorite toy, the one she was seldom parted with, the one Anton had bought for her that day in Oscar's shop. . . .

Wood splintered sharply. With his pocket knife, Oscar was tearing the ark apart. Bits of wood fell on the stone floor. Heather could hear Oscar's labored, greedy intakes of breath. He cursed angrily as he fumbled with the little boat. Malcolm's delirious words came back to Heather. *The boat*, he had said; but she hadn't listened because she had thought he was in a dreamworld. This was the boat Malcolm had been talking about! Heather stared as the toy fell apart in Oscar's hands.

"Ah," he grunted, flinging away the last pieces of wood. In his palm he held a little sack made of chamois leather. Calmly and with great precision he shook the contents of the bag into his other hand.

In the wavering light of this subterranean room, drawing fire from even the black dancing shadows, they glittered: the Mogul Stars. Heather had never in her life seen diamonds such as these. There were more than a dozen of them, and they lay in Oscar's palm like shards of rainbow.

Everyone seemed to have stopped breathing. Their eyes were wide and filled with answering fire, as they stared, hypnotized by the stones.

Oscar closed his fingers over the treasure. "All right. They're here. That's all that matters." He dropped them back into the chamois sack, and shoved them into his pocket. "We've got to get out of here now. And fast. This place is no longer safe. You may have observed that hole over there in the ceiling.

"Well, Miss Ashley here, who owns the house, led us to that. It goes right upstairs would you believe? After all these years . . . . But we must get out. We are, as they say, discovered."

Geraldine gave Heather a venomous look. "I wonder how she ever figured such a thing out? Stupid little snip. She's managed to spoil quite a few things."

"Shut up, Geraldine. There's no time for your catfights," Oscar snapped. "Get going, all of you, back the way you came."

"What about them?" asked Max, pointing at Heather and Susie. "What'll we do with them?"

Heather held her breath.

"We can't take them with us," Oscar said. "Tie the woman up," he decided impatiently. "The kid can't go far on her own. Here use this." He produced a rope, and Max pinned Heather's arms to her sides, while Jacques tied her hands and feet. Heather struggled helplessly. They shoved a filthy rag into her mouth to gag her. Roughly, they laid her out on a crumpled tarpaulin, and plunked Susie's inert body down beside her.

"They'll find you in no time," said Oscar as he turned away.

"Papa, if she tells the police—"

"I'm not worried about the police, my dear. I have never worried about the stupid police. It is the others in our little network, the ones on the other side. If they learn we've made off with these stones . . . . But it is my biggest score ever, my retiring gesture. No one shall be allowed to ruin it for me. Let us go!"

And they filed out of the room taking their lights with them. The flashlight glowed and faded away in the tunnel with the receding footsteps.

Heather was left in darkness. She wrenched and twisted her wrists and ankles, but she was hopelessly bound. It was no use. She strained her ears, trying to pick up Susie's shallow breathing.

The child stirred. Thank goodness! She would come out of it soon, Heather hoped. But not here, not in this terrifying suffocating black room. She must get loose!

She struggled again, with the frantic energy of desperation. The rope tore and scraped the skin on her wrists, but it didn't loosen. Jacques had done a good job.

Hot tears started in Heather's eyes. Of all the stupid things she had ever done, to bring Oscar *with* her, to walk calmly into his lair! But he was the last person in the world she would have suspected.

So Oscar, sweet old Oscar the village toymaker, was a crook—a criminal mastermind, shadowy and clever, as Malcolm had said. Unbelievable! But nothing was believable these days. Nothing was what it seemed to be. . . .

Except Anton. Anton was strength and sanity. Oh, where was he? *If only someone would come!* Heather wished desperately.

Then she heard footsteps coming along the tunnel. A little slowly, a little cautiously . . . and there it was, yes, a bobbing light. Nearer and nearer the footsteps came, and Heather raised her head, straining to see.

The light flashed into the room, bounded off the walls of the dark chamber, picking out the stone floor. It shone on Heather's eyes, momentarily blinding her.

A shadow person came to them across the darkness of the chamber. Heather could not quite see. . . . Hands fumbled with her gag, and let the flashlight rest beside them, so that Heather's eyes recovered . . . Celine?

The person untying her, working with swift,

competent fingers, was Celine! Heather's mind couldn't question this, not now.

Celine didn't speak, but kept working on the rope at Heather's ankles, while Heather, twisting her body, bent over Susie. She listened to her breathing, her chest. It was regular, this small sweet breath, whispering in the darkness. There was no asthmatic wheeze.

They had drugged her all right, but had had the sense not to overdo it. Heather's tears this time were tears of relief.

Footsteps pounded again in the tunnel, and above their heads on the staircase. Shouts, orders, more lights. And suddenly Anton was there. He was on his knees beside them, clutching Susie to his chest, with his eyes fastened on Heather's in terror and gratitude.

"Take her," Heather said with a wan little smile. "I'm all right."

With one powerful arm, he took her around the shoulders and raised her to her feet. "Come on," he said hoarsely. "You're coming with me."

HEATHER NEVER REMEMBERED the exact details of their stumbling progress along the old tunnel; of the crooks being herded off by a large force of police. Her one anxiety was to get Susie outside into the air.

Two days later Malcolm explained.

He was sitting up in his hospital bed, pale and bandaged, but cheerful. Heather and Anton regarded him with concern, but he brushed this aside.

"Wounded in action, that's all," he grinned.

"Part of my job. I'll get a big promotion, cracking this case. And *you*," he added nodding at Heather, "should get a medal."

"No, I shouldn't. All I did was muck things up, and get in the way."

"Well, you helped by getting yourself locked in the old house overnight. You convinced me there was definitely something suspicious about the place."

"Who was in there by the way? Did the police find out?"

"Seems to have been one of the rival factions in the gang—the ones Oscar and his group were trying to split away from. They really believed they could have those diamonds all to themselves, you see. But the other crooks were having none of it, and I guess they suspected something about the old house, too. The secret chamber was Oscar's private preserve. He's been using it since the war. Discovered it by accident one day while mending something in the cathedral. The tunnel, as you know, leads from there to the subbasement of the Savorin house."

"One of those leftovers from the witch-hunting days," Anton commented.

"Right. I told you it wasn't all legend. Anyway, everyone but Oscar had forgotten about it. He used it to hide things in during the war, and then he turned to contraband and smuggling. He worked with thieves, getting things out of Switzerland. But he kept the upper hand. He never told them where he hid things, or how he got them out of the country. Only a few cohorts were in on it—including Geraldine.

"Geraldine, as you now know, is Oscar's daughter," Malcolm added. "She is also Celine's daughter."

Heather clapped her hands. I suspected that much, but did you ever think, Malcolm, that Celine would turn out to be on our side?"

Malcolm and Anton both laughed. "Frankly, no," Malcolm said. "But you can't hang people just for having bad manners can you?"

"I'm puzzled," Anton said. "What is her story?"

"It's a bit like something out of a Greek drama. Years ago Oscar and Celine were—involved. Celine became pregnant, but he wouldn't have anything to do with her. She went away to France, and nobody in Sion ever saw her again until recently. But she knew a lot about Oscar. . . . As we discovered, she had once been involved in petty crime herself.

"When she had this illegitimate child she became thoroughly reformed, even something of a fanatic. She spent several glum years raising Geraldine to become a pure, moral example.

"But Geraldine, being her father's daughter, rebelled. As soon as she could she took off. This was during her teens. She made her way in the world, and eventually came to Sion to trace Oscar.

"He, of course, couldn't acknowledge her publicly. He was the white-thatched old toymaker by now, a kindly fixture in town.

"So she called herself Dumas, and then—"

"Then met me," Anton interjected. "She became Mrs. Valdemar. For a while . . . ."

Heather squeezed Anton's hand. Malcolm watched them, his face expressionless. Then he spoke again.